THE ROAD TO EVER AFTER

THE ROAD TO EVER AFTER

MOIRA YOUNG

Illustrated by Hannah George

MACMILLAN CHILDREN'S BOOKS

First published 2016 by Macmillan Children's Books

This edition published 2017 by Macmillan Children's Books
an imprint of Pan Macmillan
20 New Wharf Road, London N1 9RR
Associated companies throughout the world
www.panmacmillan.com

ISBN 978-1-5098-3256-9

1 3 5 7 9 8 6 4 2

A CIP catalogue record for this book is available from
the British Library.

Printed and bound by CPI Group (UK) Ltd, Croydon CR0 4YY

For my father, with love and gratitude

'It is not down in any map; true places never are.'

Herman Melville, *Moby-Dick*

There are times that are blind to such as angels. There are towns that are blind to them, too.

If – by some chance or high design – an angel had tumbled from the blue, it would have lain, unseen, in Brownvale's dry gutters till its mighty wings parched into dust.

The times were, indeed, just such times. And Brownvale was just such a town.

The Angel Maker

Davy emptied the brooms from his bag. He laid them on the ground according to size. Made of twigs, grass and feathers, there were twelve in all. He used the largest ones for smoothing the earth in preparation and broadly sketching the outlines. The smaller grass and feather brooms were for finer detail.

He made his angel pictures in the early dawn while people slept. He'd done a small one already that morning, in the patch behind the doctor's. He was setting up for his second in the front yard of the parsonage. It was risky. Parson Fall had a fearsome temper. But his yard was the largest, flattest space in town, with the earth raked daily by an odd-job man. It was so perfect for making pictures, it was irresistible. As was Davy's itch to make pictures in the dirt.

He didn't take this risk very often. Today he would.

The dog sat on the pavement outside the wire-mesh gate. He watched Davy's every move with lively interest.

'You can't come in,' Davy whispered.

The scruffy black-and-white terrier had begun to follow him the day before. Davy didn't recognize him from the pack of hardened Brownvale strays, and he wasn't confused, like a dog recently dumped. He had a hopeful kind of air about him, an apparently confident expectation that someone – Davy, for instance – would soon adopt him. He gave a sharp little bark.

'Shh!' Davy cast an anxious glance at the parsonage. But the window blinds remained down.

Parson Fall's iron heart held great sway in Brownvale. His large congregation lived under his rule. Liquor and dancing were forbidden. The only hymns they sang were those that he himself composed. His black-clad figure was a familiar sight, striding Brownvale streets with zealous energy, sharp-eyed for the smallest transgression. He sat on every board and committee, from the court right down to rubbish collection, and would always turn the business to his way of thinking. If a man could be said to be a looming dark cloud, the Parson was the cloud that darkened Brownvale.

But he did have the best yard for making pictures.

And Davy lived below the Parson's radar. Davy lived below the notice of most of Brownvale. A mousy-haired, dark-eyed boy of medium height without home or family was not memorable in any way. And Davy took particular care to move around the edges of town, so as not to draw attention to himself.

No one knew he was Brownvale's angel maker.

He made his pictures everywhere, on any flat bare patch of ground. Not benign, smiling angels though. Davy drew the mighty archangels. Heaven's high warriors of awe. The Archangel Michael overthrowing Lucifer, for instance. The twisting power of their bodies. The vengeful fury of Michael's sword raised high to strike. His pictures splashed like riots upon the ordered streets of the town.

Turn a corner, take a stroll, dash out for milk, you just never knew. Where there had been none the day before, there one would be. An avenging angel. Judgement. Revenge from above. How people took them depended on how uneasy their conscience was that day. They might halt dead in their tracks. They might look up in alarm at the sky above or avert their eyes and scuttle past like a nervous crab. Parson Fall had made Brownvale that kind of place. So, despite their beauty, the angels were widely disliked. It might be thought a parson would approve of fiery angels, but Parson Fall did not. His conscience was uneasy, like all the rest.

Davy didn't mean to poke at anyone's conscience. He simply copied paintings from the reference book in the library, *Renaissance Angels*. Had there been a selection of painting books Davy would have ranged more widely, but there was just the one. As it was, he preferred the archangels to any other. Their warrior fierceness gave him heart.

He rubbed warmth into his hands. So close to Christmas, the mornings were chill. Then, with quick strokes, working quietly, he used his largest twig broom to smooth the ground.

The dog whined. Davy dashed to open the gate and pick him up. 'You have to be quiet,' he said. The dog took that as his cue to lick Davy everywhere.

Then Davy heard it. A rumbling on the road, headed his way. White lights raked back and forth across the dawn grey sky. His heart slammed and he ducked back into the yard to hide. He crouched under the laurel bushes, clutching the dog to his chest, his hand clamped over its muzzle. 'Shh,' he whispered.

Davy waited and waited, barely breathing. Then a battered, filthy truck rolled slowly past. Roaming searchlights mounted on a rack on top of the cab scoured the sky and the ground. Davy cringed back from their scraping brightness, pushed himself deep into the waxy stiffness of the laurel leaves.

Mr Kite, the gangmaster, was behind the wheel of the truck. Day or night, you never knew when he might be roaming Brownvale on the hunt. Vagrants and homeless down-and-outs were his quarry. Young or old, it didn't matter. So long as they could work, Mr Kite would snatch them and sell them on. The Town Council, well pleased to be rid of these vexing problems, slept easier in their beds thanks to Mr Kite.

He steered with one hand, oh so casual. His jaws churned a plug of tobacco as his head turned from side to side, following the track of the searchlights. A bloodhound drooled next to him on the seat. Behind them was a rack of tranquillizer guns. In the cage on the truck bed several figures crouched, clinging to the bars. They'd been too slow or unwise or just plain unlucky. A cold shiver ran over Davy's skin.

He held his breath till the rumble of the engine disappeared and the lights faded once more into dark, then he crawled out from the bushes with the dog. Dodging Mr Kite was a regular challenge.

Davy returned to his picture. He'd planned which one he would sweep at the parsonage today. No archangels. No, he would sweep something gentler. Something more suited to Christmas. Tolmeo's *Angels Among the Magi*, from page fifty-two of *Renaissance Angels*. But he wanted to try another painting first.

He'd seen it only once, the day before.

The cold wind billowed Davy's jacket as he leaped up the stone library steps. Slapping through the door, he found it quiet as usual. Apart from the library bums, that is. The little gaggle of Brownvale down-and-outs were there, as always, keeping warm.

Howard had set up camp by the revolving stand of paperback romances. Feet up on his duffel bag, reading glasses perched on his nose, he was engrossed – as he was most days – in a tattered copy of *Forever Amber*. Except today he was holding it upside down. Davy had to say his name twice before he looked up. Howard peered over his glasses. 'I can't make head nor tail of this darn thing,' he said.

Davy turned the book the right way up. 'There you go – page ninety-two. You're at the bit where she goes to jail.'

'Jail!' Howard's eyes popped with surprise. 'A nice girl like that?' Howard had big holes in his memory and

11

it seemed the plot of *Forever Amber* had tumbled into one of them and got lost.

Though Davy lived his life on Brownvale's sidelines, he did have his own small circle of society. Mainly Mr Timm and the library bums, and Miss Shasta Reed, who ran the Bellevue picture house on Main Street. Plus a few elderly folk he odd-jobbed for.

Mr Timm was busy packing history books in cardboard boxes. Davy slipped around the counter into the librarian's private room to wash his hands in the cracked china basin. Mr Timm's little room always felt too personal. The fraying collar and cuffs of his overcoat on the hook. The onion sandwich in wax paper on his desk. After drying his hands on the thin roller towel, Davy headed back into the main room, plucked *Renaissance Angels* from the 'Reference Only' shelf and took it to the study table.

There was a free chair next to Jewel. The oldest of the library bums, Jewel had a chin full of hairs and a shaking complaint that gently wobbled her head all the time. Her lips moved as she read a children's picture book. Her crabby finger kept her on track. 'I like to read,' she told Davy as he sat down.

'Me too,' he replied. He began to turn the heavy pages. Francesco Maffei. Brueghel the Elder. Raphael. The name of the painting, the artist's name and some dates. Mr Timm called those things the 'attribution'. There was a full-page colour picture for each painting. Davy lingered so his eyes could drink them in, memorizing each little detail. He stopped, frowning. He'd never seen this one before. Three times a week for the past four years, that's how often he'd studied *Renaissance Angels*. But, until that moment, he'd not noticed this particular painting.

It was a night scene in a forest. A man stood watchful guard on a body. He wore no armour, not like the archangels did. He had neither wings nor a halo. But he was a warrior, formidable, like them. Tough and battle-hardened, his hands gripped the pommel of his sword. By his side was a magnificent hound, the size of a small pony, with a rough coat and a noble head. The pale body they guarded was maybe that of a friend or a comrade, laid out in death on a great stone slab.

The colours were dark and sombre. The dog and the man stared out of the picture, eyes straight ahead. There was something odd about them. What was it? Davy peered more closely. Yes, whichever way he shifted, their eyes seemed to follow him. There was a challenge in their steady gaze. A direct challenge. As if they knew him and expected something from him. It was unsettling. It was unlike any other painting in the book. Davy looked for the attribution, but there was none. No title, no artist, no dates, not a word. Just the painting, speaking for itself.

He took it to the counter. Mr Timm was checking off a printed list. Davy spoke to his bald patch. 'Something's happened to the book,' he said. 'It's not the same.'

Mr Timm inscribed a tidy tick. And then another.

'There's a page I never saw before, it wasn't there till now. Another painting. Everything else is where it was, but –' Davy held out the book – 'it's different, Mr Timm. Is it a new one?'

'New!' Mr Timm looked up. 'When did I last have money for new books? Money for anything, for that matter? Cast-offs, donations, paint peeling off the walls . . .' He flicked a despairing hand at the stacks.

Only then did Davy see that the shelves were noticeably thin of books. It seemed that, faced with Christmas closing, Brownvale readers had been borrowing the maximum eight allowed.

'It's just that it's changed,' Davy said. 'I mean the book, *Renaissance Angels*. Mr Timm? Are you OK?'

The librarian had taken off his spectacles to pinch the bridge of his nose. He smiled wearily as he said, 'I'm just tired, son. Come back tomorrow, tell me then.'

Davy frowned at the picture he'd just swept in the Parson's yard. He'd done it all wrong. The warrior on guard ought to have an air of expectation, of active waiting. And the hound . . . He hadn't got him right either. But the more his mind's eye tried to see the unexpected painting, the more hazy and far away it became. He needed time to study it properly.

He grabbed the large broom and brushed it all aside under the laurels. Then he smoothed the earth for his planned picture, Tolmeo's *Angels Among the Magi*.

With Mr Kite gone, Brownvale was once again quiet. Davy stood in the winter dawn and closed his eyes. He brought the Tolmeo to his mind and set it there. Then he sent it flowing through his body and began to sweep.

He swept swiftly, in a kind of rush. Bending, turning, reaching. It was as if his brooms were part of himself. He'd done the Tolmeo enough times that his body remembered it. That's how it always seemed to Davy, anyway. That the paintings, once learned, stayed inside him.

And though he was sweeping nothing more than the dry brown earth, he imagined pulling colours down from the eastern dawn sky. The haze of pink bleeding into grey, turning purple. Deep scarlet, brilliant yellow, burnished gold. From his eyes, through his body, down his fingers into the earth and into the picture he was sweeping. The hues melting and shifting. The light glowing. Dirt was dirt, Davy knew that, but he felt that his pretending somehow gave his pictures extra life.

He'd shut the dog out of the yard again after Mr Kite had passed in his truck. While Davy swept, it had been running back and forth, whining. Now, just as Davy finished, the dog leaped the gate. He flew at the broom in Davy's hand, seized it and took off.

'No!' hissed Davy.

He chased after him around the side of the parsonage and down the service path where the dustbins were kept. In the Parson's study, the blind was halfway up. The lights were on. As Davy went to grab the broom, he saw the Parson through the window.

He was there in his study filling a hip flask from a

whisky bottle. His movements were brisk, as if he'd done it many times before. The flask full, he slipped it in his back trouser pocket. After a quick nip from the bottle, he hid it inside a hollowed-out book. The book went in the bookcase, which he locked with a flourish before hiding the key above the door. Davy stared, open-mouthed. Parson Fall was a secret drinker. What a two-faced old humbug. What a fraud.

The dog dropped the broom and barked. The Parson looked up at the noise and saw Davy there, standing at the window. Davy turned to run and hit the dustbins. Metal crashed, the dog yelped and Davy's quiet life in Brownvale exploded.

Davy ran, in a panic, back to the yard to collect his brooms. As he scrabbled on the ground, the front door shot open and spat the Parson out. With one leap he vaulted the steps and grabbed Davy by the collar. Davy went flying to his feet. A slight boy of thirteen was no match for a grown man, and the Parson had been an amateur boxer. Mindful of the early hour and his wife asleep upstairs, the Parson leashed his fury. 'Shut up that dog,' he said.

The dog stopped his noise at Davy's frantic hushing. 'I didn't see anything. I swear I didn't,' Davy said.

Parson Fall thrust his unshaven face into Davy's. With sour whisky breath he hissed fiercely, 'You are gone. From this moment. Understand? I'm calling Mr Kite and if he finds you, by God you'll wish you'd left town when I told you to.'

Mr Kite. Davy had dodged him once today already. His luck might not hold out a second time.

'Please, I won't tell anyone, not ever,' Davy said.

'So it's been you all this time. These damn angels everywhere. Even here in my yard, right under my nose. What do you mean by it?' The Parson shook him hard. 'What do you mean?'

The dog began to bark again.

'Nothing, I swear it,' Davy said.

A blind snapped up smartly. A window slammed open. Startled, Davy and the Parson looked up. Mrs Fall leaned out from her upstairs bedroom window. She was in curlers, wrapped against the chill in a woollen housecoat and shawl. 'Parson Fall,' she said. 'Explain yourself, sir!'

The transformation was instant. Quite something. Slipping a friendly arm around Davy's shoulders, the Parson smiled in fake fatherly concern. 'The boy's little dog went in the dustbins, my love. I was anxious to quiet him, my dear, before he woke you.' His tones oozed oily servility while his arm tightened like a vice around Davy.

Mrs Fall said to Davy, 'The Parson's concern for my welfare is directly proportional to his need for my money.' She looked down at *Angels Among the Magi*. 'So you're the one who makes the angel pictures.'

'Yes, ma'am,' he said.

She gestured him forward. The Parson shoved him to go and stand beneath her window. Davy looked at her curiously. Mrs Fall was rarely seen about town. It was said that marriage to the Parson had made her a chronic invalid. She was certainly thin and pale, with a fretful, pinched face, but her voice was strong enough. Her words stabbed sharply at the morning air and the Parson winced, like he could feel every one.

Mrs Fall's frown softened as she gazed on Davy's picture. 'I saw the real thing once,' she said. '*Angels Among the Magi*. When I was a young woman, I made the ocean crossing with my father to the old countries. We visited the great museums and important sites of culture.' She turned her eyes to Davy. 'This is very like, apart from the colours. How do you know all these paintings?'

'I copy them from a book,' he said.

'What is your name, angel boy?'

19

'Davy David, ma'am.'

'Take my advice, Davy David. Don't spend your life sweeping dirt. In the meantime, though, you're welcome to make angels in my yard. Mr Fall won't have paid you, the Parson is a philistine. A Tolmeo angel at his feet and he'd sooner step on it,' she said. 'Hold out your hand.'

Davy caught the coin she let drop. It was heavy.

'Thank you, ma'am. Thank you!' He collected his brooms, shoving them into the bag any old way.

Mrs Fall glanced at the sky, pulling her shawl around her more snugly. 'There's a wind on the rise,' she said. 'You're without your coat out of doors, Mr Fall, sir. Do oblige me by catching your death.'

Throwing his wife a look of pure dislike, the Parson slammed back inside. With a dry smile of triumph, Mrs Fall let her window down.

Davy shouldered his bag and hurried from the yard. As he urged the dog out and turned to close the gate, he saw Parson Fall standing at the front window, staring at him. Davy flinched. The Parson's face was dark with plans for retribution.

The matter wasn't closed, Davy knew it. He'd have to work out pretty quickly what to do.

*

Mrs Fall was right. The wind *was* on the rise.

A breeze brisked through the front gate and circled the parsonage yard. It nosed around the edges of the Tolmeo magi, then moved on. Like it was in search of something quite particular.

Under the laurels it found what it was seeking. And what it sought was the raised ridge of earth, the swept-aside leavings of Davy's forest scene, the strange picture of the warrior and his dog.

The breeze lifted a drift of that earth and whisked it off down the street. Past the whispering church, the library's murmur and the bakery's yeasty warm breath. Past the hum of the movie house and the buzzing window of First Electric, with its TVs that few could afford.

It came upon the little black-and-white dog, sitting on his own. The breeze kicked him with a bit of dust to make him sneeze and, with a quick nip at his tail, hurried on.

It flew the earth from Davy's picture over to the far edge of town, where Main Street became the road east to other places. It flew it to the boarded-up museum, a tall gingerbread villa from Brownvale's prosperous days. Its girders groaned with tiredness from holding up the walls. Creaks crept along its floors and up and down the stairs. The glass-cased exhibitions, forgotten by the town, sighed as they dreamed of their living times.

The breeze dashed up the path and slipped under the front door. It set its dusty load down in the entrance hall. And there, on the chequered tiles, the earth began to whirl in an urgent dance.

The church clock was chiming nine when Mrs Taft, the Falls' daily help, left by the parsonage back gate. She came along the lane with an armload of grocery bags, passing the wall where Davy lay in wait. He slipped out from behind it and began to follow. Hearing his footsteps, she glanced back. When she saw it was him, she went faster. But the wind was snatching at her skirt and in her struggle to stay modest, she stumbled and dropped her bags. There was a crash of glass.

Davy ran to retrieve the cabbage and potatoes that went rolling. Her cheeks were pink as they gathered what had spilt and repacked the bags. Wordlessly, Davy handed her a parish calendar for next year. He chased down a sheaf of paper headed with the parsonage address. Judging by the sudden strong smell of perfume, the broken glass had been a bottle of scent. Mrs Taft had been pilfering from the Falls. Davy took the bags and, side by side, they proceeded in silence through the breezy morning. Old newspapers slapped against dead lamp posts. Rubbish tumbled in confusion at where to go.

Davy had never seen Mrs Taft close up before. She was almost pretty, though fading fast. It was a fact that Brownvale husked people early. The place seemed to suck on their youth, draining them dry like a thirsty desert traveller. Davy thought of Mrs Taft's husband, laid out just three months ago in Field & Sons' viewing parlour. Davy had sneaked in to see for himself what the town whispered of on every corner. And his skin, like all of theirs, had crawled in delicious horror at the sight of Ben Taft lying in his coffin and the heavy drape of black silk carefully arranged where his head ought to have been. He'd had it kicked off by a cow out at the slaughterhouse.

At last Mrs Taft spoke. 'Parson Fall will have the gangmaster after you,' she said. 'If you've got any sense, you'll leave town like he told you to.'

'I won't tell about the liquor, I swear,' Davy said. They walked on for a bit, then he said, 'Would you speak to him on my account?'

'And why should I?' Mrs Taft stared straight ahead, not looking at him.

'I live here,' said Davy. 'I always have. Where would I go?'

'It's nothing to me where you go,' she said. 'You and them angels. Oh yes, he told me. They don't bother me, of course,' she went on, tossing her head. 'Unlike some, I'm glad to say *I've* got a clean conscience. What d'you want to go sweeping pictures in the dirt for, anyways?' There was real curiosity in her tone.

Her question gave Davy pause. He'd never had to find the words to say why he swept. At last he said, 'It's this feeling, inside of me. I *need* to make pictures. I just have to.'

Her lips thinned to a tight line. 'We all do what we have to,' she said.

Davy thought about what he could say next, how he could persuade her. The toes of their shoes kept time together as they walked. Hers were worn just about as badly as his. Her stockings had been mended many times.

'I see plenty around town,' he said. 'What folks get up to, I mean.'

She walked quicker, her head held high. Her cheeks were flushed.

'But I keep what I see to myself,' he said. 'Please, would you speak to the Parson? Would you speak for my character to him?'

'I'm sorry, but I can't,' she said.

Davy didn't want to say what he said next, but she'd left him little choice. 'You and him, I've seen you kissing,' he said.

Her face was burning now. 'Parson Fall's pledged to marry me,' she said. Davy didn't know much about such things but it seemed unlikely. Though he said nothing, she sensed his doubt and bristled. 'Oh yes, he will,' she said. 'It's for certain. Just as soon as that wife of his does the decent thing and dies.'

They'd reached Boxcar Row, the railway sidings filled with rusting boxcars abandoned when the railroad went bust and the trains stopped running. Davy knew this part of town, but had never had cause to visit until now. It was common knowledge that Mr Taft's death had left his family on the skids. Mrs Taft must have moved here to keep a roof over their heads.

Limp clothing danced jigs on the drooping washing lines. The wind rattled the flimsy stovestacks in tinny song. People went about the everyday business of cooking and washing and talking to their neighbours, but Davy sensed a sullen hopelessness in the air. Mrs Taft was one of the few lucky ones, with her job at the parsonage. She made for a boxcar where a skinny boy of eight or nine stood lookout at the open door. He held a thumb-sucking baby hitched on his hip.

Davy hauled her grocery bags up the makeshift steps and followed her inside. 'If I happen to see a thing, I can just forget it right away. I'm no snitch, ma'am,' he said. 'Parson Fall holds you in such high regard.'

She had a quarter section of the boxcar at the front partitioned by furniture and flimsy curtains. It was gloomy within, but Davy could see enough. They would have been getting by all right before with two wages coming in, but Ben Taft's death had brought them down. There was a mattress, a tin trunk and a camp stove on a folding table. The broken perfume couldn't hide the smell of cabbage and damp bedding. Inside a crate, a little girl hugged a torn cloth dolly. Her dirty napkin sagged to her knees.

'Peter, for pity's sake, change Cora's didie,' said Mrs Taft. 'And wipe her face, can't you see the child's nose is a crust?' She chided him further for not meeting her eyes, saying he'd get nowhere with such a hangdog look. Davy felt sorry for the boy. There was an oil lamp but Mrs Taft didn't light it. She tied an apron over her dress and began to unpack the bags.

Davy stood there, wondering whether he should offer to help. Her frown told him not to. Beyond telling Peter off, she had no words for her children. The three of them watched her silently, their eyes following her every move.

'I never asked for anything, not till now,' Davy said. 'I've been shifting for myself since I was your boy's age.'

'All right, all right, I'll speak to him,' said Mrs Taft. 'Now I'm busy, you'd better go.'

'Thank you, ma'am.' Davy jumped from the boxcar to the weed-choked track below. He peered back inside, shading his eyes from the sun. 'The Parson . . .' he began, then stopped himself. He was about to tell her he didn't think that Parson Fall could be trusted, but who was he to say? Mrs Taft was a grown woman. She knew her own business.

In the front yard of the parsonage, the wind was busy underneath the laurels. It whisked another drift of earth across town. When it reached the museum, it nudged its dusty load to join the whirling dance underway in the hall.

Mrs Taft would speak to the Parson. Davy's feet took him lightly back into town. He'd wait a day or two for things to settle, then he'd sweep another picture for Mrs Fall in the parsonage yard. She'd said he was good, maybe she'd pay him again.

Pay him. Mrs Fall had given him money! What with all the fuss, he'd almost forgotten. He put a hand in his pocket to feel the coin's friendly weight. Surely his luck was on the up.

He kept half an eye out for the dog. After the ruckus he'd caused, Davy had chased him off. He hated having to shout at the creature. The dog had looked so tragic. But Davy couldn't afford any more trouble.

As he walked, the Taft children began to burden his heart. And he felt the heat of shame for his low methods flush his face. It was no better than blackmail when you got down to it, telling Mrs Taft he knew about her and the Parson. She had those kids to think of, where Davy only had himself. The coin was suddenly unbearably heavy.

When he got to Main Street, he went straight to the Christmas toy booth in the square. There he pondered the selection of wooden toys, all painted in cheerful colours. The man, who was not from Brownvale, was helpful. 'Babies like,' he said, shaking a rattle. 'I dye with vegetable so when baby suck, it make no harm.' Davy chose one and, with the man's help, a caterpillar pull-toy for the little girl. He agonized over his final choice, picking up one thing, then another. It seemed to Davy that, of the three, young Peter was in most need of a gift and Davy wanted badly to get it right. At last he said to the man, 'It's for a boy, about nine. If it was you, what would *you* like best?'

The man looked at Davy, then gave a nod as if he understood. Their heads met as they both leaned over the toy display. 'OK, I am a boy, I have nine years. Not this one, not this. Ah,' said the man. 'Here. The red yo-yo. This is very special, the one we want.'

He took care parcelling the gifts neatly in brown paper and string. Davy borrowed a pencil from him, brand new from the stall. *Baby Taft. Cora. Peter. Merry Christmas*, he wrote. Then he drew a small angel on each one. 'You are artist,' smiled the man. 'Please, keep the pencil. A gift from one artist to another.'

Christmas had brought the travelling holy book hawkers and apocalypse pamphleteers to town. Their loud hectorings tangled in the air. Davy paused at the shabbiest of them, who was resting from his labours, sitting on the pack that contained all he owned. The last time Davy had seen him, back in the summer, he'd been predicting The Rapture for September. But here it was Christmas and the world seemed likely to carry on. 'Hey, Mr Helm, it's me, Davy,' he said. 'We're still here. Guess you'll have to carry on with your pamphlets for a while yet.'

At the sound of Davy's voice, Mr Helm's milk-filmed eyes turned towards him. 'We ain't here for long, Davy boy. Not for long.'

Davy crouched down and rustled the stack of pamphlets, as if he were taking one. 'You sold many today, Mr Helm?'

Mr Helm's reply was swift. 'There's none so blind,' he said fiercely, 'none so blind as they who will not see.'

'That's for sure.' Davy took his hand and pressed coins into it. 'Here you go, I'm taking six. For Christmas presents.'

Mr Helm pulled him in close. 'The angels are gathering. I can hear their wings,' he whispered. 'I speak to them, but they never answer. If they speak to you, will you ask? Ask if they got a message for Levi Helm.'

'I will, sir,' Davy said. 'Merry Christmas.'

Mr Helm passed through Brownvale several times a year, with his badly printed pamphlets warning of the end of the world. In Davy's opinion, no angels would be coming to save anyone any time soon, but if Mr Helm believed otherwise, who was he to say?

Christmas meant more people than usual had their personal effects laid out to sell. Shoes and clothing, bits of furniture, kitchen goods. Davy had it in mind to replace the perfume Mrs Taft had dropped and broken. The woman selling her dresses, dancing on hangers in the branches of a tree, also had a bottle of French perfume. Her hands were eager, tugging out the stopper for him to sniff. Her two skinny kids clung to her legs. He felt bad, but it was down to the dregs and the label was worn. Instead, he bought from a sharp-eyed hawker selling new boxed colognes from a suitcase. Davy had to show the man his money before he'd spray the demonstration bottle for Davy to smell.

He was well pleased with his purchases, making his way among the other shoppers, listening to the Brownvale brass band trump out carols. For the first time, he had an armload of gifts to give out. For once, he was a bit like other people. He spent the last of his money on a plain bread roll, which he ate as he whistled back to Boxcar Row.

Davy leaped the library steps two by two. There'd been only the baby and little Cora, asleep in the crate, when he'd returned to Mrs Taft's boxcar. Of Mrs Taft and the boy, Peter, there was no sign. Davy had tiptoed in and out again, leaving their presents piled on top of the tin trunk.

He made a beeline for Mr Timm's room to wash his hands, then went to the 'Reference Only' cart behind the desk. But *Renaissance Angels* wasn't there. In fact, not a single book was on the cart. Puzzled, Davy looked around for Mr Timm.

He spotted the librarian in the science section, clearing a shelf of books into a cardboard box. Rushing in, so intent on his mission, Davy had not noticed what was now obvious. He turned in a slow circle with rising alarm. Almost every shelf was empty of books. An uncommon rush of borrowers for the Christmas holidays could not account for it.

He hurried to Mr Timm. With a plunging feeling in his stomach, already knowing that it wasn't so, Davy said to him, 'Is the library being painted?'

Mr Timm patted his shoulder with awkward concern. 'Let's sit down in the office, son. I brought us doughnuts.'

The doughnuts lay forgotten on the side of the desk, seeping jam into their thin bakehouse bag.

Davy took the news in silence, though he felt his ears flame red and his chest go tight. The library was to close. When it closed for Christmas, it would close forever. Something to do with the Board and the budget and no money. Mr Timm was being forced into early retirement. He'd be moving out east to share costs with his sister in her apartment. He gave Davy a full explanation of the whys and wherefores, but Davy couldn't really take it in.

'What about Howard? Where will he go?' said Davy. 'And Jewel only just learned to read. That's down to you, you taught her. Does the Board know that? Did you tell them?'

'I'm afraid people don't fit on their balance sheets,' said Mr Timm.

'Then their balance sheets are wrong.'

'I offered to go on half-pay.' The librarian spread his hands in helpless resignation.

'You've got to fight them, Mr Timm! You can't give up,' Davy said.

'The fight's over, son. Their minds are closed. I'm truly sorry.' They were silent. Sitting there, hunched, Mr Timm seemed to have shrunk inside his shabby suit.

'What'll happen to the book?' Davy said at last.

At that, Mr Timm perked up a little. 'Ah. Well.' With a wink and other gestures of conspiracy, he unlocked the bottom drawer, took out *Renaissance Angels* and placed the book on his desk. 'I've managed to lose this in the paperwork. It's yours now,' he said.

Davy stared, shaking his head. 'I can't. It's stealing. You'll get in trouble. *I'll* get in trouble.'

Mr Timm thought for a moment. 'I know what.' He rummaged for a pen and an old receipt book, fished a few coins from his pocket and shoved them over the desk. 'I always searched out your pictures on my evening walks. I especially like the archangels.' At Davy's start of alarm he smiled. 'Oh, your secret's safe with me. Go on, take it. I only wish it could be more. Now, what you do with it –' he looked over his spectacles at Davy – 'is entirely up to you.'

Davy caught his drift. 'I don't suppose that book's for sale, Mr Timm,' he said.

The librarian pretended surprise. 'Why yes, as it happens, it is. And I see you've got the exact money. I'll just write you a receipt, and I'll stamp it right here, and that makes it all official.' He tore it off with a flourish. 'You are now legally the owner of *Renaissance Angels*. I know you'll use it wisely. I have faith in you.'

They stood, Mr Timm gave him the book and they shook hands. Head down, Davy dashed around the desk to hug him with a fierce and sudden love. 'I'll never forget you, Mr Timm.'

After Davy had gone, Mr Timm sat there for some time, thinking. It was small, the light he'd held for all these years. But he'd held it steady to show a path through the darkness. Now it, too, would be extinguished. Still, he had reason to hope. For there was Davy. The boy already shone. And one day, thought Mr Timm, he would surely blaze.

Davy ran home to the graveyard with the book wrapped in his jacket. As a rule he didn't run. A running boy might attract notice and he was always careful not to draw attention to himself. But he was anxious to stash his treasure. The size and weight of it made him feel conspicuous.

His place was as good, probably better, than any safety deposit box. He entered the graveyard his usual way, through the loose fenceboards behind the tiny chapel. There was no one around as he swung the boards back into place.

He made a brief stop at an out-of-the-way section unmarked by any headstone. Known to Brownvale as Potter's Field, it was the bit of ground set aside for the burial of paupers, orphans, vagrants and suicides. Davy had been told his mother lay somewhere among them, the unnamed girl who'd traded her life to give him his. In the absence of knowing exactly where she'd been buried, he'd claimed a spot in the corner as hers and planted a briar rose to mark it. He retrieved the hidden milk bottle that he kept filled with water and now, crouching, he watered the rose's roots. After four years of careful attention, it was still struggling to establish itself in the dry soil.

'Hey, Ma, you'll never guess,' he said. 'That book I told you about? It's mine now, all mine. I own it. Look.'

Along one edge of the graveyard stood a line of yew trees, bowing and bending in the wind. They'd been growing side by side for so long that their branches had entangled them together. In one place, that entanglement had formed a hollow, a kind of den that Davy called home.

The air around the yews was bright with bird voices. Davy shared the trees with a clan of sparrows. He'd been in the graveyard one spring day shortly after the Home's closing had left him on the street. Watching the birds coming and going as they fed their young, he'd realized that a nest was a thing of wonder and thought one might well do for him, too. It would surely beat living in an alley among the dumpsters.

In the four years since he set up home, he'd become friendly with his feathered neighbours. Now he pushed into the hollow among the branches. His nest was snug and dry and dark, lined around with cardboard, with two sleeping bags for warmth. Davy quickly wound up his flashlight. The book was really his, he could scarcely believe it. He immediately flicked to where he thought he'd seen the mysterious forest scene with the warrior and the hound. It wasn't there. But he had no time now to look properly, that would have to wait until later. The book went into the drawstring bag in which he kept his few belongings.

He tucked the bag deep into the branches, next to the potato sack with his brooms, then hurried off to find some work so he could eat.

At the parsonage, the breeze snatched at the last of Davy's swept-aside picture. Urgently, as if there were a waiting train it had to catch, it raced the dust across town to the museum and threw its load upon the chequered tiles.

It could do no more. The rest was down to others.

They were all elderly folk on their own, the ones Davy would call on to see if they had any odd jobs or errands going. Between the handouts and small coins they gave in payment, he just about managed to sustain himself.

But he was out of luck today. '*What a shame . . . if only you'd come yesterday. Maybe after the holidays . . . try me then. Another boy got here early, beat you to the punch.*' Davy called on every person he'd ever worked for and some he hadn't besides, but the message was the same everywhere.

'I'm sorry, young man. Merry Christmas.' Mrs Hattie Grigg shook her head regretfully as she closed her door.

She was his last hope. Davy sloped along, kicking at the dirt and mentally kicking himself. He should have been knocking on doors first thing instead of sweeping pictures and getting into trouble. He'd just have to make do on that lone bread roll. Parson Fall's church ran the soup kitchen but everyone got herded into the chapel to be preached at beforehand, with all the doors locked so no one could bolt. Davy avoided any handout that came with conditions. Nine years at the children's home had seen to that.

He looked up and suddenly realized where he was. His search had taken him all the way to the end of Main Street, where it became the road east to other places.

The dog had shown up and begun to follow him apologetically. Davy sat on the kerb in front of the shuttered town museum. The dog sat next to him and they watched some clean-cut town boys playing kickabout on the rough ground opposite. He had no expectation that they might ask him to join in. The wind was in a mischievous mood, snatching at their ball.

Davy said to the dog, 'That was some trouble you got me into with the Reverend.' The dog stood, wagging his tail. 'Sit,' Davy said. The dog sat. 'Down,' he told him. The dog lay down. 'Why couldn't you behave before? You're bad luck, that's for sure.' The dog licked his hand. 'Don't go getting any ideas,' said Davy. 'I can't take care of you, too.'

The boys playing opposite were Davy's age, but the kind that lived in houses and attended school. Their bicycles lay on the ground, let fall from their careless hands as they jumped off. One of them noticed Davy and called to his friends, 'Hey! Keep a look out for your bike.'

Davy felt himself redden. He'd never thieved a single thing in all his life. He picked up a twig and began drawing in the dirt. He outlined the head of the great hound from the forest painting. He was just saying to the dog, 'If you saw him, I bet you'd run a mile,' when the sound of shouting made him look up. The wind had stolen the boys' ball and the game came to a halt as they watched it sail over top of Davy's head.

After a brief discussion one of them shouted, 'Hey buddy, would you get our ball?'

Such uncommon politeness sent Davy scrambling to his feet. Then he saw why they'd not chased for it themselves. And why the courtesy. The wind had flown their ball into the tangled yard of the museum.

The museum had been closed and boarded up years ago and been falling to ruin ever since. A plywood *For Sale* sign lay rotting by the path. Braver kids would sometimes edge through the gate on a dare, especially at Halloween time. But mainly everybody kept away. It was said that an old witch lived inside.

Davy hesitated. The boys shouted, urging him on. He gathered his courage and went in, followed by the dog.

The ball had lodged itself in a sprawling bush near the sagging front steps. It had been a rich man's house before the town took it for the civic museum, and a badly ripped screened verandah ran along the front and down the sides. Davy grabbed the ball and, to show he could, kicked it from where he was, flying it above the trees that choked the yard. He heard the cheers as the boys saw it coming.

'You. Young man.' The voice came from the verandah.

Davy froze. It was an old woman's voice, creaky with age. The witch! Fear tingled his skin.

'Will I bake you in a pie or drink your blood?' she said. 'Oh, I know what you all think I get up to.'

Davy turned around then, greatly daring. He could just make her out, a dark shape behind the torn screen of the verandah. It looked like she was sitting in a chair.

'You're safe enough,' she said. 'I wish to speak to you. Approach.'

With his heart banging hard against his ribs, Davy's feet moved him along the path, up the wooden stairs and stepped him through the gap where the screen door had been. The dog scampered ahead of him without hesitation.

She beckoned Davy forward. 'Stand where I can see you, just there.' He did as she said and stood in the patch of daylight that filtered through the trees. She herself remained in shadow. All he could make out was that she sat in a wheelchair with a rug tucked over her knees. The dog made himself known to her, sniffing all around. She brushed him off. 'Your name?' she demanded of Davy.

He had to swallow twice before he could answer. 'Davy David,' he whispered. 'Ma'am.'

'Whoever named you lacked imagination.' She regarded him in silence. He could feel, if not see, the keenness of her inspection. Then, 'I am Miss Flint,' she said, 'Miss Elizabeth Flint.' She began to rise, with great difficulty, from her chair.

He made a hesitant move to help.

'Get back,' she snapped. 'My decrepitude is mine to bear. I brook no interference.'

Her tone was commanding despite the quaver of age. Davy kept out of the way as she manoeuvred herself behind her wheelchair and pushed it, haltingly, towards the open front door.

Miss Flint was an ancient wreckage. Bony and beaky, like some lizard bird, she was bent nearly in half as she inched along behind her chair. Davy couldn't help but stare.

She stopped and pierced him with a look from her hooded eyes. 'Am I a wretched sight, Mr Davy David?'

He didn't want to anger her by lying. 'Yes, ma'am,' he said.

'Do you pity me?'

'No, ma'am.'

He'd clearly passed some kind of test. 'I have business to discuss with you. Come inside. Your dog may come too, if you wish.'

'He's not my dog, he just follows me around,' Davy told Miss Flint.

They had to pass through an odd whirlwind of dirt that was dancing in the large tiled museum entrance hall. Visitors were greeted by a small dinosaur reconstructed from its own bones, posed forever in mid-run on a plinth. The brass plaque identified it as *Leptoceratops*. The skeletons of other creatures were displayed around the hallway.

Davy breathed in wonder, 'You live with dinosaurs.'

'The poetic irony is not lost on me,' said Miss Flint.

The dog seemed to know how to behave properly indoors and stuck to Davy's heels. They followed her through the large main room, Davy's eyes widening at the array of items on display. Glass cases with stuffed creatures, animal skeletons, collections of butterflies and insects, rocks and fossils.

'You're the first visitor for twenty years.' Miss Flint

named items as they passed. 'Stone arrowheads of various dates, all local finds . . . Rocky Mountain locust, thankfully extinct . . . Harlan's musk ox . . .'

Davy looked around him in amazement. 'All of this here and no one sees it.'

'I was the curator when they closed it down. It suited me to stay. Keeping things in order has passed the time. Are you an ignoramus, Mr David?'

'I've never been to school,' he said.

'That's a point in your favour. There's nothing wrong with ignorance,' she said. 'The truly ignorant are more likely to be curious and open-minded. Would you say that you're curious, Mr David?'

'I guess so. I go to the library.'

'Then there may be hope for you. If you like books, you'll be interested in this.' She'd stopped by a case with a large book of old maps open on display. 'You may unlock it, the glass slides back, don't touch anything else. They're sixteenth-century, not originals of course, not in Brownvale. This is a facsimile from the early nineteenth century. Still, it's fine quality, they're all hand-coloured.'

On the open page, in each of the four corners of the map was a chubby putto blowing a blast of wind from its puffed-out cheeks. Sea serpents coiled in the waters.

Small sailing boats rode upon the waves.

'At that time large parts of the world were still unknown. Look here,' said Miss Flint, 'this little island off the coast of Ireland, Hy-Brasil. Many believed it was where the soul went when the person died. It was widely held to be there, expeditions were sent out. They never found it, of course.'

'Why not?' said Davy.

'Because Hy-Brasil does not exist, Mr David. The human race seems unable to accept emptiness, we've always invented places that don't exist. The Fountain of Youth. Valhalla. Mount Olympus. When sailors die, it's said they've gone out west. To Hy-Brasil.'

'Maybe they weren't looking in the right place,' said Davy.

'Do you have hearing trouble? I've just said it's imaginary. Lock the case and we'll proceed,' she said.

He locked it carefully. Following behind her, he had a good back view. She'd scraped her long white hair up into a messy kind of spray and stabbed it, insecurely, with a pencil. Her neck was spare as a turkey's and ringed with wrinkles of skin. Davy wondered if, like a tree, a count of them would tell her age. She wore a man's workshirt inside out and men's trousers belted up near her chest. Her feet, in canvas sneakers, splayed like

49

duck's feet as she shuffled along.

'I can feel your eyes upon me, Davy David. If you've examined me to your satisfaction, we'll get down to business.'

She led him into a small back room which, judging by the furniture and dusty shelves of files and books, used to be an office. It was cluttered, with every surface covered, but tidy in its way. There were paintings stacked against the walls. She clearly liked to read. Magazines and books were piled up on the floor. In the corner was a tiny kitchen unit with a sink and two-ring hotplate. A door led through to a small washroom. The cracked leather chesterfield was made up with cushions and a blanket for sleeping. The large window on to the backyard had dead vegetation growing through it. The dog's nose took him snuffling around the room.

Miss Flint leaned on her wheelchair, resting, out of breath. 'I need a driver,' she said. 'To take me there.'

She pointed her knobbled finger at a small oil painting, propped up among the clutter. It showed a low white house beside water. A lake, perhaps, or maybe the ocean.

Davy spoke cautiously. 'To take you into a painting,' he said.

'Are you a halfwit?'

'No.'

'Then listen,' said Miss Flint. 'The house in the painting is my destination. I need to go by motor car and I'm hiring you to drive me.' She enunciated each word crisply, as if he wasn't all there.

'I don't know how to drive,' Davy said.

Miss Flint just carried on, 'I'd like to set off as soon as possible, no later than mid-afternoon. As you can see, I'm ready to leave.' She indicated the battered briefcase lying on the chesterfield. She couldn't be taking much.

Maybe *she* was hard of hearing. Davy raised his voice. 'I'm thirteen. I don't have a licence.'

'There's your uniform.' She gestured towards a striped paper package from Warners, the men's clothiers for those with money. 'This is a journey I've planned carefully and I want my driver to look smart. The distance is just over two hundred miles. We should be there in good time. Once you've dropped me, you don't need to wait.'

Davy tried another tack. 'I don't have a car.'

'We'll take mine,' she said.

'Miss Flint, I don't drive, I don't have a licence, I'm just thirteen.'

'Nonsense.' She swatted his words away, as she would a fly. 'Nobody bothers about all that these days. Any fool can drive. If you lived on a farm, you'd be an old hand by now.'

Even if he could drive, thought Davy, he wouldn't want to drive anywhere with Miss Flint. 'I'm sorry, but I really don't think . . .' he began.

'What you think, what you think, I don't have time for what you think!' With each 'think' she thumped her wheelchair for emphasis. Miss Flint glared at him, hawk-like. 'I'm going to die on Christmas Day,' she declared. 'And I intend to die where I was born, in *that* house in *that* painting. And I intend for you, Mr Davy David, to drive me there. I'll pay you good money. Now that's an end to this discussion. Be back here no later than two.'

She thought she was going to die.

'If you're sick,' Davy said, 'I'll run and get the doctor.'

'You are a halfwit. Look!' She fumbled with the small leather bag slung across her chest, unzipping it with fingers crabbed by rheumatics. 'I'll pay you half in advance and the balance on arrival. And when we're done, you can have the car, you can keep it.'

Davy stared. 'I can have your car,' he repeated. Miss Flint might not be a witch, but she might very well be unhinged. Maybe she was having a brainstorm, like Howard from the library. He'd sometimes think he was still in the navy and go around calling people 'Captain' and start shouting if you didn't play along. Davy would have to try and get away without upsetting her.

'Yes,' she was saying, 'keep the car, sell it, do with it as you please, I won't be needing it, I'll be dead – have you been listening? It's perfectly simple – I swear you *are* a halfwit. Look here. Here's your money, half in advance.' She flapped the stack of notes she'd pulled from the bag, shaking it impatiently at Davy as if he couldn't see. In doing so, she shook her topknot loose, her white hair slithered down and then she really did look like a witch. 'What's the matter?' she cried. 'Go on, take it, it's yours!'

She flung the money and Davy stood with it blizzarding all around him. The dog began barking. Davy backed towards the door, 'I don't want your money. I don't want your car. I'm not driving you to die. Not to that place or anywhere else. I don't want your job, you old . . . witch!'

With that, Davy fled with the dog. They flew out the front door of the old museum, like they'd been blasted by a hot wind from hell. Down the path they raced, through the gate, then they were running back into town.

The boys across the road took fright at the sight of them and ditched their football game, yelling, 'Witch! It's the witch!' Leaping on their bikes, they pedalled wildly and disappeared like shots in every direction.

Shaken by his odd encounter with Miss Flint, Davy calmed himself with the noon showing of *It's a Wonderful Life* at the Bellevue. For the month of December – closed on Christmas Day – it was *Wonderful Life* at the Bellevue, four times daily, six days a week. Some wag had stolen the marquee letters so it read '_ _ s a W_ _ _ _ _ ful Life. 4 x Daily'.

Davy and the dog ducked in through the alley fire door and settled on the floor in the dark corner that was Davy's regular spot. He never sat in a seat he hadn't paid for. The carpet smelt pleasantly of soda.

Miss Shasta Reed only played old movies at the Bellevue, always black-and-whites. The screen flickered, the sound came and went and, with the blackouts, a film might stop abruptly. But Davy could lose himself there for the duration.

The first time he'd ventured uncertainly inside, the movie was playing to an empty auditorium. Miss

Shasta called down from the projection booth for him to join her. Davy found her sitting in the soft spill of light from the projector, wearing rhinestone earrings, a blue silk turban and dungaree overalls. A gold cigarette smouldered in the long holder clamped between her teeth. She was hemmed in by stacks of film cans labelled with their titles; she'd left narrow paths to squeeze along. That day's film was *Top Hat*, starring Fred Astaire and Ginger Rogers. Davy watched, awestruck, with Miss Shasta. Fred and Ginger were like beings from another world. They were radiant. Ginger's white dress flew like wings as they danced and sang with a joy unknown in Brownvale.

Davy said to Miss Shasta, 'But what about the Parson?'

With narrowed eyes, Miss Shasta blew a perfect smoke ring. 'The Bellevue was here long before he was and I intend for it – and me – to outlast him. His kind kills the spirit. We resurrect it.'

She lived in a little room somewhere in the building. She referred to it as 'my pied-à-terre'. Her audiences were sparse but she got along somehow. Miss Shasta claimed to be a heathen. From time to time, for her own amusement on a Sunday, she'd rig up speakers on the Bellevue's roof, set *Top Hat* or some other musical rolling, and blast the soundtrack all over Main Street. The game was to make the Parson come running from his pulpit. She would time him. The Parson would dance around below, shouting, and Miss Shasta would wave gaily, pretending she couldn't hear. 'I have a project to drop him dead from apoplexy,' she said.

Besides Davy and the dog, there were two people in for today's show, including the unknown man who always sighed a lot. Davy waved at Miss Shasta in the booth. She'd be mouthing every line, as she did for all her films. He found a half-full bag of popcorn in the second row, which he eked out slowly. The dog didn't care for popcorn.

The familiar story rolled out, with George Bailey ready to kill himself, believing it would be best for everyone if he was dead, and Clarence, the doddery old angel, earning his wings by showing George how things would have turned out worse if he'd never been born.

Midway through, Davy had an impulse. Keeping half an eye on the movie, he took his new pencil and began making little sketches of Miss Flint on the flattened inside of the popcorn box. He'd never sketched with a pencil before, he'd only drawn with his brooms. Wanting to sketch from real life like this was new for him. But he soon gave up in frustration. He couldn't capture Miss Flint's likeness. She was like the old house where George Bailey spent his wedding night. Both of them were all shadows and collapsing angles and weathered boards.

When the movie ended, and George and his family and friends sang 'Auld Lang Syne', Davy could hear Miss Shasta singing along up the booth. As the credits rolled, she waved him out through the fire exit.

While he'd been inside, the wind had strengthened to a gale. With the strange episode of Miss Flint fading in his mind, he headed home to the graveyard through the blowing town. The thought of being able to study *Renaissance Angels* for just as long as he pleased hastened his feet. He would decide on the picture he'd sweep tomorrow for Mrs Fall, weather permitting. This wind would be blowing today's magi picture to the four corners of the earth and beyond.

Davy vaguely heard the catcalls but it took the dog's barking and the sting of a stone hitting his neck to bring him to. He stopped. On the opposite sidewalk, two town boys stood jeering. One said, 'Yeah, we're calling *you*, meathead. Parson Fall's looking for you.'

The boys exchanged a quick glance. Davy sensed trouble and took off. They gave chase in a casual sort of way, hooting to put the frighteners up him. The dog kept running back to bark and growl at them, but Davy feared they'd kick him, so called him off. They fell back after several blocks but Davy kept running. The wind carried him along on its blast.

Davy's home was destroyed. The line of old yews was gone. Every tree was burned to a blackened, smoking ruin.

Fear clutched him. 'No!' he yelled.

They'd dragged his things out first and taken what they wanted. His flashlight was gone, his thermos flask. *Renaissance Angels* too, they'd taken the book. The scorched rags that had been his sleeping bags smouldered in the branches. They'd made a bonfire of what they didn't want. It had burned right down.

Davy grabbed a stick and dragged out the embers, shoving the dog from harm's way – but there was nothing to be saved of his belongings. His drawstring bag with his few clothes, the potato sack with his sweeping brooms, all were lost. He suddenly realized that the stick in his hand was the cracked remains of one of his brooms. They must have used them as fuel for the bonfire.

For most surely a *they* had done this. A war party. The flurry of their bootprints marked the ground.

Davy stared at the devastation. His body shuddered with shock. And as he stood there, the quiet struck him, right in the heart. His clan of friendly sparrows was silent.

'No,' he breathed. He ran to search among the blackened branches, but the birds were gone. Relief made him sag for a moment. Of course. They would have fled at the first disturbance. But if they'd had nestlings, the little things would have burned alive.

Who would do this? Who could do this to him?

Rage surged up from Davy's belly. He ran wildly here and there, yelling as he brandished the stick. 'Come back here! Get back here, you cowards!' As if those responsible might still be in the graveyard, crouched behind the headstones to enjoy his despair. But there was no one to answer. They were long gone. The stick fell from Davy's hand.

He was near to Potter's Field. He went over to his mother's little rose bush and slumped beside it. Tears were tight in his throat. But he wouldn't cry. He would not. Crying could not undo what had been done.

The dog, upset by his anger, had been shadowing Davy as he ran around and yelled. Now he trotted up and dropped something on the ground. It was Davy's toothbrush, badly scorched and useless. The dog nosed it towards him, then sat. One of his ears drooped sympathetically. His eyes were anxious and soft. Davy hugged him close to his chest.

The destruction of his life was complete. This deed was no town-boy bullying. Someone wanted him gone from Brownvale. And Davy knew exactly who that was.

RECEIPT No 3751 DATE ___

Received from _Davy David_

Dollars $ **1·00**

For _Renaissance Angels_

By _B.Timm_ Librarian

The wind staggered and tipped people along Main Street. In their flapping overcoats they looked like ragged crows against the storm. Davy spotted Parson Fall. He was swooping towards the police station with his coat-tails winged behind him in righteous vengeance. Davy's captured book was clamped underneath his arm.

'That's mine!' Davy yelled. In a rush of anger, he ran. He threw his arms wide, there on the pavement, and blocked the Parson dead in his tracks. 'You stole that,' he said. 'Give it back.' As he grabbed for the book, the Parson seized his ear and twisted it. Davy cried out in pain.

The dog began to bark ferociously.

'This boy is a thief!' The Parson raised his voice, pulpit-style, to attract the notice of passers-by. 'You may bear witness as I make a citizen's arrest, here and now. He stole this valuable book from the library, a book purchased with your hard-earned taxes for the benefit of all. He stole it for himself, the selfish thief.'

A little crowd began to gather around them. The dog was growling low in his throat.

'That's not true,' Davy protested. 'It's my book. I bought it fair and square. Just ask Mr Timm. It's mine, I swear.'

'Liar!' the Parson thundered. 'We'll march him inside to be charged.' He began to drag Davy towards the steps of the police station and the crowd followed.

'No, wait. Wait!' said Davy. 'He gave me a receipt. Look, here it is.' He fumbled it from his pocket. 'There's his signature, see? And he stamped it. That means it's legally mine.'

'Stolen property,' the Parson repeated. He snatched the receipt, ripped it up and threw it to the wind.

'No!' cried Davy.

With that, the dog lunged at Parson Fall and sank his teeth into his leg. The preacher dropped the book, screaming, 'Seize him! Get him off me!'

Davy grabbed the book. 'Come on!' he told the dog. And they ran, faster than the hard-blowing wind.

Leaving the Parson sprawled on the steps of the police station, they easily dodged those passers-by who tried to grab them. And, unlike the town boys who ran after them in gleeful pursuit, Davy had tracked cats and dogs down Brownvale alleyways to learn their larger hidey-holes and dens.

He dived into one of them with the dog. As the noisy chase hurricaned by, Davy held his breath, trying to calm himself and work out what to do. Miss Shasta. She'd shelter him at the Bellevue. But then what? Make like Lon Chaney in *The Phantom of the Opera* and lurk inside the movie house for the rest of his life? Drag Miss Shasta into his troubles? No, that wouldn't do. He was someone who solved his own problems. One thing he knew for certain was that he couldn't hide like this for long, scuttling rat-like from nook to cranny around the town. They'd be calling Mr Kite to hunt him down. Once his bloodhound caught Davy's scent, that would be it.

After a time, his panic eased. His mind cleared. There was one way out of this and only one. Davy's life that he'd built with such care the past four years – his life of library, movies, odd jobs and errands and, above all, his angel pictures – that life of being his own man in Brownvale, it was done.

He had to leave town today and not come back.

Davy hauled great handfuls of rampant vine from the garage door. He was hampered by the stiffness of his new uniform. In his opinion, he looked ridiculous. Like Norma Desmond's chauffeur in *Sunset Boulevard*, in plus-fours, a fitted jacket and a shiny-brimmed cap. It didn't help that it had been made for someone much larger. He tugged and squealed the door open along its rusted track.

He stared in dismay. Miss Flint's car was a crank-start saloon. A few old-time autos still hacked around town, relics from the ancient past of cars just like the ancient fossils who drove them. He might have known. 'Does it run?' he said.

Miss Flint flapped an irritated hand. 'Load up, hand me in and we'll get going. We'll have to leave the wheelchair. I'll manage on my sticks.'

Hurrying, Davy put their meagre luggage in the boot. He stowed Miss Flint's leather briefcase and the cloth bag she'd given him, which held only his burned toothbrush and *Renaissance Angels*. Then, with the aid of her two sticks and much gasping and irritation, Davy somehow got her inched from the wheelchair to the car. After wrestling with the bulk of her fur coat – a moth-eaten rug, so far as he could tell – Davy heaved her into the back seat and she was in.

Settling herself royally on the cracked green leather, Miss Flint righted her fur hat, which had been knocked turvy with the fuss. She glared sourly at him, a real lemon-sucker of a look. Her entire face puckered with disapproval. 'There's room for improvement,' she sniffed. As he slammed her door, she snapped, 'Don't slam the door!'

Davy cranked the engine nervously, ready to leap out of the way. He'd watched old-timers crank-start and knew these cars were inclined to kick in protest, but to his surprise, the engine caught right away. He ran and hopped into the driver's seat. 'Now what?' he said.

Miss Flint explained the brake and gas pedals and rattled impatiently through park, reverse, neutral and drive. She told him about the mirrors. Then she made him repeat it all back to her. 'Now,' she said. 'Take off the brake.'

Davy lifted his foot. They bunny-hopped forward.

There was a horrible crash of something metal. 'Reverse,' she shouted. He clashed the gearshift and stomped on the gas. They shot backwards into the lane. 'Brake, you fool! Brake!' yelled Miss Flint.

Davy laid his head on the steering wheel, gasping for breath. 'I don't think I can do this,' he said.

'Nonsense. We're already late. Forward, driver, through town. Our way lies west.'

Cautiously, Davy cranked the steering wheel to turn them around, bumping first into a wall then the garage. As he wavered them down the back lane, the car bucked and coughed like a smoker clearing phlegm.

'Not both feet, you foolish boy. One at a time, brake *or* gas.'

Their road out lay on the far side of town. He drove them crookedly along Main Street. Crossing pedestrians leaped for the safety of the sidewalk. No matter. The faster Davy got away, the better. Parson Fall would be looking for him. Davy imagined being hauled bodily from the car.

As the thought crossed his mind, Parson Fall stepped in front of the car.

'Brake!' yelled Miss Flint.

Davy braked and froze, his heart pounding in his chest. But the Parson didn't see Davy. He didn't even glance his way. He was too deep in plotting dark deeds with the man beside him. It was Mr Kite.

His bloodhound snuffled the ground, straining strongly at its leash. In Mr Kite's hand was Davy's best shirt. They'd taken it for his scent. The Parson's trouser leg was torn, his bandaged calf visible through the tear. As the two men hurriedly crossed the road, the preacher was limping badly. A gang of tumbling town boys paraded behind them, giddy with malicious excitement.

The blood pounded in Davy's ears. His hands were claws on the steering wheel. They hadn't seen him. Four feet away and they hadn't seen him. They were looking for Davy David. But only where they expected to find him. Not behind the wheel of a car, dressed like a movie chauffeur.

'I'd say whoever they're looking for is long gone,' said Miss Flint. Davy met her gaze in the rearview mirror. 'We're attracting attention. Drive on,' she said. With a shaky breath, he pressed the gas pedal and they were off again.

They passed the Bellevue, where Miss Shasta in her blue silk turban balanced atop a ladder replacing the stolen marquee letters. Outside the library, Mr Timm, with a hammer and tacks, was posting the notice of closure on the door. His sparse hair haloed his head as he turned to greet Howard, toiling up the steps for his daily read of *Forever Amber*. Davy bid them all a silent farewell.

The gale whirled dust devils around their turning tyres. It wheeled people's hats away down the street. Past the church they went, past the parsonage where Davy's downfall had begun that morning. Then they sailed past the town limits and they were gone. Gone from Brownvale for good.

They were on the road now, on a journey to the sea.

The Road West

They'd gone perhaps a mile or so. Davy had slowed considerably, down to a crawl. He clutched the steering wheel, concentrating hard to keep them going straight. Driving was unnatural. He didn't care for it at all.

Miss Flint was complaining from the back seat. 'You're like a tortoise, creeping along, I've booked a room for the night at a reputable inn. At this rate, we won't get there till next week. Look out!' she cried.

They hit a pothole and bounced out. He wrestled the wheel to keep them on the road.

'I plan to die calmly and on schedule. I'll thank you not to shake me to death. Still, no need to dawdle. Step on the gas.'

'Step on the gas,' Davy repeated. He dared to press the pedal a little more. People drove all the time. He'd surely get the hang of it soon. 'Gas, right,' he muttered to himself. 'Brakes, left. Park, reverse, neutral, drive. Mirror.' He'd forgotten what she'd told him about the

73

mirror. He glanced over his shoulder, 'Miss Flint? What did you say about –'

'Eyes front,' she barked. Then, 'Brake!'

Davy thumped both feet on the brake as something white streaked across the road in front of them. The car rear-bucked and stalled. In the sudden, awful quiet, he saw a small dog lying on its side.

Davy scrambled out and ran. It was the black-and-white terrier. His eyes were closed.

'No!' Davy fell to his knees beside him.

At the sound of Davy's voice, the dog's eyes opened. His head lifted. His stubby tail gave a feeble wag.

Miss Flint rolled down the window. 'Is it dead?' she called.

'I think he's hurt,' Davy said.

'Hurt? At that funereal pace?'

With uncertain hands, Davy felt the dog's body. 'I can't see any blood, but I'm not sure what to –'

'Oh, for pity's sake!' She managed to creak open the back door, but couldn't get herself out. 'What's the matter with you? I need assistance. Don't just gawk.' Davy ran to help and got another lemon look when he knocked off her hat. But he got her going on her walking sticks and followed as she thumped her slow way over to the dog.

'He's been following me around,' Davy told her.

He helped Miss Flint lower herself to the ground and, with what seemed to Davy an experienced touch, she examined the dog with care. He licked her hand. 'Never mind your fuss,' she said. 'I think he's all right. Probably just in shock. We need to keep him warm, though. Let's have your jacket. Come, come, Mr David.'

Reluctantly, Davy slipped it off. He covered the dog, then helped Miss Flint to her feet again. She leaned on her sticks. They stared down at the dog. He looked up at them. His stubby tail wagged in a hopeful kind of way.

'He's an undistinguished beast,' said Miss Flint. 'I can't recall, do fleas live throughout the winter?'

'Fleas!' Davy mourned for his new jacket. 'He bit Parson Fall on the leg.'

'Good for him. I'm surprised he wasn't poisoned. Well, pick him up. He'll have to sit in front with you.'

'He's coming with us?' said Davy.

Miss Flint was caning a slow, breathless path back to the car, with her fur coat dragging behind. 'We can't leave an injured animal,' she said.

Davy scooped the dog carefully to his chest, carried him to the car and laid him on the front passenger seat. He settled Miss Flint in the back – 'Don't slam the door!' – then got the engine cranked and running once again. When he climbed in behind the wheel he found the dog sitting up. His ears were perked, his tail a flurry of delight.

'You faker,' said Davy. 'That was an ambush.' He reached over, threw open the door and said, 'Go on, get out.'

'Ambushed. By a dog.' In the back seat, Miss Flint began to wheeze. Davy turned, alarmed that all the excitement might have killed her. Her face was creased, but not in pain. She was laughing rustily. 'Like a highwayman,' she said. 'He's got character, I'll give him that. Let him stay.' The dog barked. 'There,' said Miss Flint. 'You're outvoted.'

Davy kicked the front bumper, batting at the billow of steam from the engine.

Miss Flint leaned from the window. 'What's the problem, driver?' Her tone was tight with irritation.

Davy muttered, 'It's a hundred years old, that's the problem.' He raised his voice, 'I don't know, but I nearly burned myself to death just opening the bonnet.'

'Not the radiator again. Let me see.' He helped her out and she caned around to peer through the clouds of steam. 'The man swore to me he'd fixed it,' she said, coughing. 'Aren't people just the living end. It's the modern way, completely unreliable.'

Davy's suspicions were roused. 'When did you have it fixed?'

'Oh, recently. Five years ago? Certainly no more than seven.'

'Seven?' he said. 'Well, what do you expect?'

'What I expect,' she said, 'is for a job to be done properly.'

The evening was gathering against the winter afternoon. The light went early this time of year, the shortest day had only just passed. Davy shivered and buttoned his uniform jacket right to the collar. It was crumpled from the dog sitting on it. It was peppered with dog hairs. And, possibly, most distressingly, with fleas.

The dog had barked furiously when the steam first billowed out. Now, deeply suspicious, he kept a rumbling growl going as he eyed the hissing car.

'Can we fix it?' Davy asked.

'If you were a proper chauffeur, I expect you could.'

'I told you I can't drive. You hired me, Miss Flint.'

'And now I wish I hadn't. You're too slow, too erratic, you know nothing about engines, and look at you.' She waved a hand. 'You're not even smart, you're covered in dog hair.'

He stared at her in disbelief. 'You're the one who told me to wrap him in my jacket.'

'I don't like your tone, Mr David.'

'I don't like yours much,' Davy said.

'You're fired,' said Miss Flint.

'Oh no, I quit.'

Davy let the bonnet drop with a crash. Then with a show of pleasure that made her glare, and with great deliberation, he went around slamming all the doors. The boot stuck. He thumped it open and snatched his bag. As an afterthought, he took out her suitcase. Then he marched to the roadside and stuck out his thumb.

She'd paid him half his wages, more than he'd ever had in his life. He'd hitch a ride somewhere, take a bed in a hostel, maybe even rent a room in a boarding house for a time.

He did his best not to watch as she crabbed off slowly on her sticks. How had she managed on her own in that museum? Still, she had, hadn't she? And how Miss Flint chose to live – or die, for that matter – was nothing to do with Davy David. She began to inch her case towards the road by pushing it with her sticks.

'Good grief,' Davy muttered. He went and grabbed it and put it by the road. Then he set himself up again, but well in front of her. He'd take the first ride. She was on her own. He squashed the thought of old women out alone in the night and robbers cruising back roads for breakdown victims. They were on a sleepy back road, for sure. No cars, no street lamps, not a sign of any house. Woods on either side. Where *were* they?

He glanced over his shoulder. Miss Flint stood with

her thumb out, looking like some odd kind of bear in her moth-eaten coat and hat. She pretended she didn't notice him and leaned to look out along the road.

The dog sat halfway between them.

Some time passed. They did not speak. Restless, Davy opened *Renaissance Angels* to search for the painting of the forest scene. But again, he couldn't find it. He collected some twigs and made a Raphael in the dirt. The dog stole one of the twigs, wanting to play, but Davy chased him and took it back. He rubbed out the Raphael and made a witch with a pointed hat. It looked very much like Miss Flint.

He heard an engine approaching. He quickly scrubbed the ground and got to his feet. A truck rocked into view. As it neared, Davy squinted at the sign above the cab. '*Webb's Poultry! Freshest! Finest!*' he read aloud. Then he was hit by the sound. The towering load was a host of turkeys crammed into crates, furiously gobbling as they headed for their doom.

'Yup, they're stupid all right,' shouted Mr Webb. 'You know when it rains? They're so amazed they stare up at the sky, but they keep their beaks open, see, so they fill up and drown theirselves. Can't get much stupider than that. That's why you gotta keep 'em inside.'

'Tosh.' Miss Flint said it to the window but Davy heard. He sat wedged between Mr Webb's ample flesh and the bulk of Miss Flint's fur coat while the dog lounged in comfort on his lap. Straw and feathers whisked around the cab and out the open windows. But no amount of fresh air could mask the sharp ammonia of the droppings Davy had felt squash beneath his boots as they climbed in.

'But dogs, now you're talking, I like dogs,' Mr Webb was going on. 'What's this fella's name?'

Davy looked at the dog. What *was* his name? 'George Bailey,' he said, to his own surprise.

'Dog with a last name. Mighty fancy, just like your suit.' Mr Webb leaned around him to address Miss Flint. 'Grandson, huh? Got two of 'em myself. Can't abide kids. That's the wife's department.' He shifted gears noisily as they rounded a bend.

'I know just how you feel, Mr Webb.' Miss Flint treated him to a vinegar smile. 'Again, thank you for stopping, so kind. That service station you mentioned, is it far?'

'Not that far, no. Anyways, so they hang 'em up by their feet and clamp their necks and off they go on this conveyor, all the way around the shed. The scenic route, I like to call it. Scenic!' Mr Webb chortled in delight. 'So then,' he continued, calming down, 'they clank along till they reach the knives, then it's chop-chop, head-off, just like that. It's modern. Real efficient. Stupidest birds on the planet, turkeys.'

They drove on with the turkeys gobbling frantically to each other in the back. Miss Flint said, 'And they're alive all the time?'

'Yup.'

'They can see what's happening?' she said.

'Like I told you, they're stupid, they got no idea,' said Mr Webb. He suddenly pulled off the road on to the gravel and set the brake. 'Duty calls,' he announced. Leaving the truck running, he squeezed himself from the cab and hurried off into the trees.

Davy and Miss Flint sat silently with the newly christened George. After a moment, she said, 'Odious man.' After another moment, she said, casually, 'I don't suppose you could drive this thing?'

A look passed between them.

'I'd need a hand with the gears till I got the hang of it,' Davy said.

She held up her knobbled hands. 'Will these do?'

Davy dumped George and slid into the driver's seat, still warm from Mr Webb. Miss Flint shifted over to sit next to him. Together, they slotted the gearshift into drive. Davy released the brake and hit the gas. They took off fast, spitting gravel as he bumped the truck back on to the road.

Miss Flint grabbed the hanging strap. 'I hope those crates are tied on!'

Furious yelling came from behind them. Davy glanced in the wing mirror. Mr Webb rushed from the bushes clutching at his trousers. He gave chase, red-faced and shouting. For a man who waddled, he was pretty fast. But he quickly gave up. They left him leaning over, gasping for breath.

Davy thumped the steering wheel, whooping in triumph as George Bailey barked his excitement. 'Did you see that? Turkey vengeance! I'm the Archangel Michael!'

'Eyes ahead, Mr David. Concentrate on your driving.'

Miss Flint sat, looking serene, as if she stole a load of turkeys every day. She waited until Davy got to grips with driving the truck and George calmed enough to stop his barking. Then she quietly gobbled. After a moment, Davy gobbled back.

They looked at each other and they smiled.

Miss Flint tapped the crate with her stick and the startled turkey shot out. 'Off you go, shoo! A Manhattan, Mr

David, consists of whisky, sweet vermouth and bitters. I don't know why I never had one. I intended to this evening, but events have overtaken us. It can be served in a cocktail glass topped with a maraschino cherry or on the rocks, as a lowball.'

Davy thought. 'I think Bette Davis drank one of those. In *Now, Voyager*,' he said.

'You know, I think you might be right.' Miss Flint looked at him with interest. 'You go to the Bellevue?'

'Sure,' he said. 'I even pay sometimes.'

Unloading the truck and coaxing all the birds from their crates had seen the night close in and Miss Flint's schedule fall apart. Davy urged out the last one. 'Go join your friends,' he told it.

As it stalked off to explore its new surroundings, Davy stood to enjoy what they'd done. The abandoned fruit orchard was full of turkeys, clucking and chirping. It was just the males that gobbled, according to Miss Flint. Some flapped about uncertainly, many were already at roost on the lowest branches while others roamed beneath the trees for wizened windfalls.

'No one's worked this place for years,' she said. 'They'll be safe from people at least. Once they trim down, they might even get flying.'

'So it isn't true? I mean, what Mr Webb said about turkeys in the rain.'

'An old wives' tale, the man's a cretin,' said Miss Flint. 'And I would have told him so if we hadn't needed the ride. The wild turkey was a noble fowl. Sadly extinct now, of course.'

'Miss Flint, can I ask you a question?'

'I'm sure you can, but yes, you *may* ask me a question. I might answer or I might not,' she said.

'Why me?' said Davy. 'You could have hired a real driver. There're plenty of people looking for jobs.'

'Just count yourself lucky,' she said. 'If not for me, you'd be in Mr Kite's hands by now.'

They took a last look around. 'Do you think they know they're free?' said Davy.

'I should think so. They're intelligent creatures.'

George had shown little interest in the turkeys and bedded down in the truck early on. He yawned widely and shook himself as they got back in and started up.

'For the sake of my nerves, do not grind the gears,' said Miss Flint.

Davy ground the truck into gear with an ear-wincing clash. As they pulled away, jolting and bumping, Miss Flint leaned out the window and called, 'Good luck! Merry Christmas, my feathered friends!'

Miss Flint leaned on her sticks, pausing to get her breath. They looked up at the burned-out neon sign. The New Inn offered *Liquor! Pool! Eats! Rooms!* 'I don't know about reputable, but it'll have to do,' she said. 'I'm sure they can mix a Manhattan.'

Davy doubted that, but knew she wouldn't thank him for saying so. He glanced at the stolen truck, parked in the darkest corner of the tavern's quiet lot. He could just make out the little white blob of George, staring out through the back window. Miss Flint claimed to know vaguely where they were. It was blind luck they'd happened on the place when they did. And it was safely miles away from where they'd abandoned the turkey farmer.

Davy held the door for Miss Flint as she caned her slow way in, with her fur coat dragging behind her. Only then, in the light, did he notice that she was feathered with turkey down and quills. So was he. He hastily picked off what he could as he followed her inside.

The tavern was one barn-like room. As they entered, the roar of voices ceased and every head in the room turned to look at them. They were men, working men. This was not at all the kind of place for an elderly woman of Miss Flint's stripe. Or for a boy dressed like a movie chauffeur. Someone wolf-whistled and Davy reddened. Another clucked like a chicken. The men laughed and then got back to their evening's business of drinking and boasting and shooting pool.

They made for the only free table, in a corner. It was crowded with dirty drinking glasses. Miss Flint tutted. 'Waiter!' she beckoned. As they sat down, Davy shrank inside his jacket and clutched the bag with his book to his chest.

The barman came to them so slowly and with such surly disdain, it was evident he'd never been summoned before.

'A Manhattan cocktail, waiter,' said Miss Flint, in her grandest voice.

'A Manhattan,' the barman repeated. From his tone, Davy knew he'd never been asked for one before. And, from the calculating look he gave Miss Flint, Davy could tell he knew she'd never had one. She ordered Davy a soda float. The barman clanked up the glasses.

As he swiped the table with a careless rag, he sized her up, in her fur coat and hat. 'You want to run a tab?'

'A tab,' mused Miss Flint. 'Yes, why not? What's on your menu this evening?'

Silently he indicated the hot dog machine where two lonely frankfurters turned in slow rotation, impaled on the greasy wheel of spikes. Judging by their state of shrivelment, they'd been there for some days.

'We'll take two,' said Miss Flint. 'And we'll need rooms for the night. One superior suite with bath and one economy single.'

'A superior suite. Of course, madam.' The barman clicked his heels and left.

'This isn't so bad,' said Miss Flint. They took in their surroundings, scarred by years of hard use and bare of any decoration, apart from a faded poster of the last king of England, rudely defaced and being used as a dartboard. *It's a Wonderful Life* played, unregarded, on the television mounted behind the bar. The only other nod to Christmas was the Santa hat limply lidding the jar of pickled eggs.

'Do we go back for the car tomorrow?' Davy asked.

She shook her head. 'We're wanted criminals. I'll have to rearrange our schedule accordingly.'

Davy was facing into the room. It meant that, along

with the drinkers ranged on the stools at the bar, he could watch the barman make Miss Flint's Manhattan. Bottles of liquor were lined up and sniffed. Half a dozen were poured from, freely, then stirred with a pencil from behind his ear. The barman bowed as he delivered the drinks, then twirled his tray on one finger as he sauntered back to the bar.

Davy's soda float was soda with a single ice cube, though he knew it should include ice cream. Miss Flint coughed considerably at her first sip of Manhattan, then pronounced it nice and just as she'd imagined. The hot dog managed to be both dry and greasy, and the bun was stale, but Davy ate with gratitude. He'd not eaten anything since his popcorn at the Bellevue. 'You never answered my question,' he said.

'Don't speak with your mouth full. You've asked me a number of questions. Which one in particular have I failed to answer?'

'Why me?' said Davy. 'When I turned your job down, why didn't you hire someone else? You were ready to go. What if I hadn't come back?'

She leaned over the table. 'Why do you sweep angels in the earth? Wasting your time and effort on something people scuff with careless feet. Something the wind blows away, that no one wants or asks for. Oh yes, Davy

David, I know you're the one who makes them.' She leaned back again. 'I've seen you.' she said.

'You have?' said Davy.

'When you're my age, you don't sleep much. I like the time before dawn. Until last year, I used to get about a little, when other people weren't around. You were, though. Why do you make them?'

He'd been asked the same question twice in one day now. He thought for a moment, then said, 'Miss Shasta – you know, at the Bellevue?'

Miss Flint nodded.

'She eats, sleeps and breathes movies. That's what she says. I think it's the same with me and my pictures.'

'A true artist makes his own pictures,' said Miss Flint.

Davy was stung. 'I do,' he said. 'I mean, not that often, but sometimes.'

The barman appeared at their table. With the martyred air of someone mightily put upon, he delivered two more drinks, saying, 'From Mr Bunting. He's picking up your tab.'

'I'm not acquainted with a Mr Bunting,' said Miss Flint.

They looked over to the bar. A man in a rumpled suit sitting alone at one end, raised his glass in salute.

'He's a crook,' the barman said. 'The respectable kind, a lawyer.'

Mr Bunting received a frosty nod from Miss Flint. Alone again, they sipped their drinks. She didn't want her hot dog, so Davy wrapped the flimsy paper napkin around it and put it in his bag to give to George. He realized she still hadn't answered his question, *why him?*

But before he could ask again, she began to quiz him. Was he an orphan? Abandoned? 'I knew they closed the children's home,' she said. 'No one wanted to adopt you? Take you for a factory hand? Or farm work?'

'I guess not,' he said.

She scrutinized him closely, not something he was used to. He shifted uneasily, but he held her gaze. 'I can see why,' she said at last. 'The first impression is that you're ordinary, just a boy. But then one notices that your eyes are far too *seeing*. And that makes you not ordinary, but odd. I expect you make people feel uncomfortable.'

Davy took no offence. He thought she might be right. 'So if you're going to die, what's wrong with you?' he said. 'Can't they operate or give you medicine?'

'I need no medicine,' she replied. 'I'll tell you this, Davy David. Elizabeth Flint has lived far too long to no good purpose. By rights, she should have died years ago.'

For a moment, he couldn't think how to reply. 'If you didn't like it, you could have killed yourself,' he said.

She gave a mirthless bark of laughter. 'You're forthright, at least.' Then she said – and it was if she were talking to herself – she said, 'I guess I kept thinking it would all amount to something. But the years just went on.'

'So, are you sick or not?' he said.

'You're very slow, Mr David. Think. What do you suppose this is all about?'

He shook his head.

'When we get where we're going, there will be a coffin waiting,' she said. 'It will have a brass plate engraved with my name and dates. The date of my death will be two days from now, Christmas Day. My eightieth birthday. It's all arranged, all paid for, very simple. I'll lie down in it, I have some pills that I shall take and . . .' She shrugged. 'Does that answer your question?'

Davy nodded. She was matter-of-fact. The prospect of being dead in two days' time apparently did not disturb her at all.

She took another sip of her drink. 'I don't suppose this is an appropriate conversation for such early acquaintance. Still.' She roused herself to a smile. 'You have seeing eyes and we are partners in crime.'

Davy yawned hugely. Too late, he remembered to

cover his mouth. 'Sorry,' he said. 'I never had such a busy day before.'

'It's been full of incident, I'll grant you that. I'm quite tired myself. Get our room keys from the man.' Miss Flint gave him money to cover the room charge.

The crowd at the bar was several deep and Davy had to press through with determination to get where he'd be noticed. On the TV above the bar, the movie had reached the bit where Clarence the old angel was explaining to George Bailey that every time a bell rings, an angel gets his wings.

Hotly self-conscious, not wanting to sound foolish, Davy made himself raise his voice to claim the barman's attention. 'Can I have the keys to our rooms, please?'

The barman gave him a hard look. 'I got one room,' he said. 'For the old dame, not you.'

Davy paid. As the barman rang the sale into the register, the cash drawer sprang open with a ding. On the TV screen behind the bar, Nick, the movie barman, was doing the same. He rang his cash register over and over, saying, 'Hey! Get me! I'm givin' out wings!' Davy stared up at the screen.

The barman slapped the key on the bar. 'Oi! Looky Lou! This ain't no picture palace. Door over there, top of the stairs.'

Mr Bunting, the lawyer who'd paid their tab, was still sitting alone at the far end of the bar. As Davy headed back to Miss Flint, he called Davy over. His rumpled suit was rusty with age, his hair a tangle of frizzy, greying curls. Altogether, he was frayed around the edges, a shambling kind of man. He had a nice face though, Davy thought, open and calm. Mr Bunting sipped his drink, a root beer, through a straw. His bright blue eyes looked straight into Davy's and Davy found himself saying, 'Do I know you?'

Mr Bunting smiled. 'You look like you're on your way somewhere. With the lady?'

'Yes, sir.'

Mr Bunting regarded him for a moment. Then he nodded and began to search his pockets. He pulled out a coin and handed it to Davy. 'Some places only take the old money,' he said.

The large copper coin was worn and bent, the markings almost worn away. It was like something from Miss Flint's museum. Davy looked at Mr Bunting, puzzled.

'Keep it handy, just in case. You never know,' said Mr Bunting. 'Merry Christmas, kid.' He went back to his root beer.

Davy stood there for a moment, then pocketed the coin, saying, 'Thanks. Merry Christmas to you, too.'

*

Davy didn't quite know how he got Miss Flint up to her room. There was no handrail. The staircase was narrow and dark. He somehow had to pull and push her at the same time. He caused her pain without meaning to. She cried out sharply once or twice. He apologized over and over. 'Just get on with it,' she said. He didn't want to think how he'd get her down again in the morning.

At the top of the stairs, Davy unlocked the door and found the light switch. A naked bulb ticked into life. It was an attic bedroom, being used as storage for a lean-to of folded chairs, stacked tins of cooking oil and other things. The iron bedstead was made neatly with a blanket. An orange box hosted a bedside lamp. The blocked fireplace huffed cold draughts of winter into the room. The filthy window smeared the moonlight coming in.

He helped Miss Flint over to the bed and clicked on the lamp. Their breath steamed in the chill. Her laboured gasps worried him, they seemed too loud. 'You should probably keep your coat on,' he said.

Miss Flint pulled off her hat. In the harsh light overhead she was hollowed. Fragile as the dead sparrows he would sometimes find in the graveyard.

Davy asked if she wanted anything. She waved him

no. He placed her walking sticks within reach, said goodnight and made to go.

'Briefcase,' she said suddenly. 'Painting. Photograph.'

The first thing that Davy saw when he opened the case was the small brown pharmacy bottle containing her pills. *Warning. Do not exceed the recommended dose*, the label read. These were the pills she'd told him of. The ones she would use to kill herself. This was real. She could really do it. Impulsively, he slipped the bottle in his pocket.

She gestured impatiently.

'Sorry,' he said. 'Yes. Here they are.'

The painting was the one she'd shown him, of her old home by the sea, their destination. And he noticed the childish signature of the artist, E. Flint.

The framed photograph was in beside the painting. It lay on top of a banded stack of money. The image had faded ghostly pale down the years. A boy and girl stood at the open door of that very same house. Two summer children like those in Brownvale who rode bicycles and battled giants as they outran the days all season long. He wore shorts. She wore a thin cotton dress. Their friendly arms and legs entangled as they smiled, squinting, at the photographer. A small terrier a bit like George sat at their feet.

'Was this you?' said Davy.

She didn't answer. 'Just there, where I can see them,' she said.

He propped the frames against the lamp and put her canes within reach. By the door, as he went to leave, as he clicked off the ceiling bulb, he saw an old-fashioned call bell drowsing there.

She said his name and Davy turned. 'For the absence of doubt, I'm unfiring you. I need a driver,' she said.

'Why me?' said Davy.

'You sweep angels,' she said. 'Isn't that enough?'

'Goodnight, Miss Flint.' In passing, as Davy left the room, his arm brushed the call-bell cord and the bell gave a gentle little tinkle.

Miss Flint picked up the photograph. She held it for some time. Then, from inside her briefcase she took a notepad and pen and, using the case for a desk, she began to write.

Once she'd finished, she got herself up from the bed. Sipping hard for air between each effort, she made her way over to the door and opened it. Then she rang the call bell for attention.

Davy woke at first light. He'd fallen asleep quickly on the bench seat of the truck, only to dream all night long. Unnerving dreams of sea-going coffins, flights of skeleton birds, and turkeys that grew on platters in the trees. His body was curled around the easy-breathing warmth of George.

They sat up, yawning, in the fogged-up cab and Davy gave George the rest of last night's hot dog. While he ate, Davy paged through *Renaissance Angels*, searching again for the forest scene that had appeared then disappeared. It wasn't there. There was no warrior with his hound guarding a body.

'I must have dreamed it,' he said. That encouraged George to climb on Davy's lap and lick his face.

The crunch of tyres on gravel alerted them. Davy rubbed a peephole on the window. A police car was pulling in to the parking lot. It had barely stopped before the doors flew open and an officer leaped out. Mr

Webb, the turkey farmer, heaved his bulk out from the other side. Davy ducked, slamming down the doorlock as he did. He grabbed his bag, and George, and dropped out the passenger side, thinking to lock that door too before silently closing it behind him.

A surprising number of cars were still parked in the lot. A fair few of them contained the inn's customers, sprawled on the back seats sleeping off last night's revels. It meant he and George could dodge around the edge of the lot and stay out of sight of the two men who were now crouch-stepping towards the truck with clumsy furtiveness. As they rattled at its locked doors and peered in through the steamed-up windows, Davy and George slipped around the rear of the inn.

The back door stood open. They hurried down a hall, past a coffee-rich kitchen that rumbled with idle chat and morning coughs. The main room was littered with the bodies of sleeping men, fallen soldiers on the battlefield of Christmas cheer. The chorus of snores didn't falter as he and George tiptoed through the doorway to Miss Flint's room.

They found her halfway down the stairs, dressed in her hat and fur coat. Her eyes were wide with excitement. 'I saw them pull in,' she hissed. 'I'm fine, you stay there.' She moved with surprising haste. When she reached the bottom, she exclaimed, 'My briefcase! I left it just inside the door.'

Davy scampered up and grabbed it. 'Follow me,' he whispered.

He had visions of running through woods and shoot-out showdowns, like in the movies. If they left the back way, there'd surely be somewhere they could hide. But as Davy opened the door to the rear hall, a man began to stretch himself on the kitchen door frame, bowing out into the hallway, talking all the while.

They hustled back the way they'd just come and soft-footed it through the main room. Mr Bunting, the friendly lawyer, was asleep on the bar. He snored with a rafter-raising gusto.

Davy unlocked the front door and sidled out to take a look. Mr Webb and the policeman were attempting to jemmy the locked truck doors with a crowbar and a length of wire. Apart from shinning up a tree, which ruled out Miss Flint, Davy couldn't see a single place to hide.

'Mr David!' He whirled around. Miss Flint was in the police car. George sat at her side. She motioned frantically for Davy to join them. He ran and jumped in behind the wheel.

'What're you doing?' he said.

'They left the keys in the ignition.'

'Oh boy,' Davy said. But he turned the key. As the engine switched on, so did everything else. The siren, the police radio, the blue light on the roof all began to wail and crackle and flash. The shock sent George into a fury of barking. Over at the turkey truck, the policeman shouted. The two men began to run.

'Which way?' said Davy. 'Quick!'

'Left! Go left!' cried Miss Flint.

He reversed the car and shoved it into drive to spin their nose around. Then Davy hit the gas. He slammed the pedal to the floor. They crash-bumped on to the road, fishtailed left and squealed off. And for the second time in as many days, Davy looked in the wing mirror to see Mr Webb yelling in red-faced disbelief. He and the policeman went running back towards the inn.

'Oh man, we're in trouble – *big* trouble,' Davy said. 'A turkey truck's one thing, but a police car – this is bad, Miss Flint, this is wrong.'

'Do as I say and we'll be fine. For pity's sake, what's wrong with this contraption?' The switches on the console were hissing and crackling, resisting all her attempts to flick them off. There was a flash as they shorted out in a shower of sparks. Alarmed, George leaped into the back seat. The roof light, the siren and the radio all went dead.

'That's better,' she said. 'Now to get back on schedule.'

How could she be so calm? His heart was jumping in his chest. 'We stole a police car, they'll put us in jail.'

'Don't be melodramatic, Mr David. They'd have to catch us first. You're an excellent getaway driver.'

A compliment from Miss Flint. That was a first. Davy glanced at her and blinked.

Miss Flint looked entirely different.

Her face, which had been a collapsed ruin of bones and hollows, was raised up and filled in and smoothed out. Her hooded eyes with their wrinkled lids, sunk so deeply in her head, were now open and clear and bright. Davy felt the hairs rise on the back of his neck.

'Good morning,' she said. 'Did you sleep well?'

He gaped, wordless.

'Watch the road,' she said. 'And close your mouth, you'll catch flies.'

Davy looked away, uncomprehending. When he'd left her last night, she'd been ancient. Barely able to breathe. And it wasn't just her face that was different. He realized how easily she'd moved as they escaped from the inn. So easily, he'd forgotten she needed help.

She said, 'We're more likely to evade capture if you put on some speed. *I* slept wonderfully well, better than

I have in years. That bed was surprisingly comfortable.'

Her back was straight, no longer bent in half. Her voice had lost that grating old person wobble. A comfortable bed couldn't possibly be the cause.

'We'll have to change our route. The police car is a complication. I think I know where we are.'

George was in the front seat again, sniffing at her and whining. Miss Flint soothed him with strokes of hands no longer crabbed by rheumatics. It would take more than a good night's sleep to remedy that.

'We'll keep away from the main roads and cut across country.' As they flashed past a road sign, she told him to bear right up ahead.

Davy kept stealing quick glances at her. In *The Great Mancini*, a hokey old movie about an evil magician, Mancini would lock his beautiful assistant in a box, make some passes with his hands and, when he opened it again, she'd turned into a dove. Davy was no magician. But last night he'd shut the door on Miss Flint and this morning she had emerged transformed.

'We'll get rid of the car just as soon as we can. We're obviously not policemen – you keep staring at me, Mr David. What *is* the matter?'

Davy tried to speak. He couldn't. Slowly, with icy hands, he turned the rearview mirror towards Miss Flint.

She went very still. She stared for some time. Then she touched her face in wonderment. Her skin and her lips. She took in the changes to her hands and moved her fingers freely, with widened eyes. Then she removed her hat and her long braid of hair tumbled down. What had been thin, white and wispy was now thick and fair, streaked with grey.

George's ears had gone flat. He whimpered.

At last Miss Flint spoke. Her voice was faint. 'I look sixty again,' she said.

Davy cleared his throat. 'You were pretty nippy back there.'

'I thought it was the excitement,' she said.

The three of them stared through the windscreen.

'This is clearly impossible,' she said.

The hour was still early, the day just beginning, when they drove into a town large enough to boast a police station. The roads were empty, the pavements too. When they found the station, Davy cut the engine and they rolled into the car park at the back. He tucked the patrol car crookedly between two others. His excited driving along narrow country roads had left the thing filthy, with an array of dents and scratches. They left the keys in the ignition and hurried off. George was visibly relieved to be back on solid ground.

Miss Flint dumped her walking sticks in the first rubbish bin they came to and strode along, upright and vigorous. 'They'll be circulating our descriptions by now.'

Davy regarded her moth-eaten coat and enormous fur hat. 'It might help if you got rid of that get-up,' he said.

She eyed him severely. 'This "get-up" belonged to

my mother.' She came to a sudden halt. She'd just caught sight of herself in a window. 'Good grief,' said Miss Flint. 'I look a wreck, why didn't you say?' She was already shrugging off the coat. Underneath she was wearing a skirt, pale pink blouse and short tweed jacket.

'Come on,' said Davy.

Down the alley over the road, he'd spotted a donation bin for clothes and shoes. The contents had been squirrelled through and left on the ground. While Miss Flint crammed her bulky coat down the chute into its guts, Davy riffled through the pile of clothing. He found a pair of trousers and a blue shirt and, ducking behind the bin, changed into them quickly. They were worn, but not too badly. Slightly big, but they would do.

He shoved the hated plus-fours down the chute and threw in his loathsome chauffeur's cap. 'Those are brand new,' Miss Flint objected. His uniform jacket was warm wool, too good to throw away. Davy ripped off the epaulettes and shrugged it back on.

'Right,' said Miss Flint. 'What next?'

Davy's stomach grumbled. 'Breakfast,' he said.

As Davy left the drugstore, the bell above the door gave a tinkle. In the diner over the road, Miss Flint was on the alert in a window booth. She waved him on urgently. George sat beside the diner entrance, beneath a sign that read *No Spitting. No Swearing. NO DOGS.* He stood, beating his stubby tail hopefully as Davy approached. 'Stay,' Davy told him. He went inside and slipped into the booth.

Miss Flint leaned across the table. Keeping her voice low, she said, 'You took your sweet time.'

'I had to buy all this.' Davy cleared the table in front of him. His waistband was tight thanks to his enormous breakfast, the only evidence of which was a swipe of ketchup on his plate and a tiny hill of toast crumbs. Davy dumped out the contents of the paper bag. A new toothbrush, tooth powder, soap, a nail brush and a comb. 'I couldn't just barge in and say, "If a lady starts getting younger, what's wrong with her?" I had to work my way up to it. I needed this stuff anyway.'

'Well?' said Miss Flint.

'He thought I was joking. Tore a strip off me for wasting his time. We need to find you a doctor.'

She shook her head. 'We're wanted criminals, Mr David.'

'But you don't look anything like you did last night.'

'They'd lock me up,' she said. '*Doctor, when I went to bed I was eighty. When I woke I was twenty years younger.*'

107

She dropped her head into her hands. 'How can this be? I don't have a single ache or pain.' She brightened. 'What about those Manhattans? I did drink two of them, maybe they acted like a kind of potion. An elixir of youth. No. That's desperate talk.'

'You could say it was a friend of yours, that you're worried about them,' said Davy.

'I have had one thought,' she said. 'Psychology. We've been gripped by a joint delusion. Our minds, I mean, both of us. I've read about that kind of thing.' She raised an expectant eyebrow.

A delusion. Both deluded at the same time. Davy gave it his consideration. If they *were* deluded, chances were they wouldn't know it. 'OK, so . . . how would that work?'

'You're right, it's ludicrous,' said Miss Flint. 'But whatever this is, we need to know.'

'Why?' he said.

'Why?' She stared at him as if he'd just said he could fly. 'Because this is impossible, that's why. I'm on the verge of eighty. All living things age and die, that's how it works. They don't get younger. Excuse me, do you mind?'

She glared her outrage at a man pounding the flashing jukebox next to their booth. It was taking people's money but not playing their selections. The man gave it a final frustrated thump and, instantly, it went dark.

'Serves you right,' Miss Flint told him. 'Playing jukebox music at breakfast only hastens the decline of civilized society.'

The man ignored her and went to complain to the waitress.

Davy had a sudden thought. 'Plants,' he said. 'Every winter they seem to die, every spring, they're alive again.'

'I am no Greek goddess. I am not Persephone, Mr David. Oh good.' The overworked waitress was making a hasty round of the booths, refilling coffee cups. 'I need coffee in the worst way,' said Miss Flint. 'I've been trying to catch your eye for ages, miss, but you didn't seem to –'

The waitress slapped their bill on the table as she passed with her coffee pot, completely ignoring Miss Flint.

'Well! Did you see that? Such rudeness.' Miss Flint frowned at the flickering lights overhead. 'And these lights are most vexing. They ought to get them seen to. Take note, Mr David, these are the marks of a low establishment.'

'Why do you need to know why you're getting younger?' Davy said.

'Have you practised alchemy on me? Voodoo?' Miss Flint demanded. He shook his head. 'This goes against natural law. I'm an educated woman. I believe in scientific method. There's an explanation. We just have to find it.'

She pulled a purse from her jacket and as she began to count out coins for the bill, muttering to herself, Davy pinched his arm. It hurt. He tasted the dab of ketchup on his plate. Salty sweet. He didn't think he was dreaming. He looked around the tinsel-draped diner. It smelt of fried bacon and coffee. He heard the clank of cutlery, the sound of laughter, the tinkle of the bell above the door as people came in and went out. The waitress rang up a sale on the cash register. As the drawer popped open, the bell rang.

Bells again. Bells.

'Every time a bell rings, an angel gets his wings.'

Davy suddenly sat up straight. There were bells everywhere they went. Here. At the drugstore earlier. And all the bells back at the New Inn. The call-bell in Miss Flint's room. The surly barman ringing his cash register over and over while Nick the movie barman did the same on the TV overhead. They were a message, a sign of something. They had to be. He thought hard for a moment. Then, 'Maybe it's a miracle,' he said.

110

'Hmm?' Miss Flint looked up from calculating the tip.

'This,' said Davy. 'You. What if it's a miracle?'

She positively glared at him. 'Your mind is sloppy. That's what you get for sweeping angels. There is a rational explanation for everything.'

The toaster at the counter suddenly flung six slices of white into the air. The waitress batted at them, shrieking.

'I know how to find out,' Davy said.

He grabbed her briefcase and was gone before she could ask where to. She put money on top of the bill and hurried out after him, calling, 'I've left it on the table,' to the waitress.

If Miss Flint hadn't moved so quickly now she was so much younger, she might have noticed the jukebox. How, as she passed, it lit up, vomited a clanking stream of coins to the floor and began blaring out The Delta Rhythm Boys.

'Dem bones, dem bones gonna walk around.
Dem bones, dem bones gonna walk around.
Dem bones, dem bones gonna walk around
Now hear the word of the Lord.'

And a few minutes later, she might have seen the consternation of the waitress when she discovered that the boy on his own who'd been talking to himself had left without paying his bill.

'Keep looking,' whispered Miss Flint. She blew another page over.

'Why do you keep doing that?' said Davy.

Miss Flint frowned and flapped a dismissive hand.

Surrounding them on the library study table were piles of books. Volumes of medical reference, chemistry and biology, along with branches of science that Davy had never heard of. The unfamiliar words blurred into each other as he turned page after page. It would take several lifetimes to learn everything in them.

He looked around, wishing Mr Timm could see this place. It was bustling with cheerful borrowers. Books crowded the well-stocked shelves. Where the Brownvale study tables bore the criss-cross scars of schoolboy pen-knives, these tables were smug with gleaming polish. Mr Timm would surely be cheered by this library's walls, too, with its paint that hadn't scabbed off in flakes.

Davy fiddled with the flickering reading lamp for a

bit. He stared up at the ceiling. Then he got up and headed into the stacks. George, stationed under Davy's chair, went with him.

They found a girl in a Christmas elf hat shelving books from a tinsel-trimmed cart. Its wheels squeaked as she pushed it along. She had a friendly round face. The name tag pinned to the front of her fluffy sweater said *Donna, Library Volunteer*. She'd made the 'o's into little smiling faces. 'Merry Christmas,' she said. 'May I help you?'

'Where are the books about miracles?' said Davy.

'Oh, and this one, *Mysteries of the Hindu Faith* . . .' Donna piled another book into Davy's arms. 'Hindus are very spiritual people.'

Davy had found his girl. She'd given an excited hop and tiny clap of delight at his request and dashed without hesitation to the very shelf. She ran a finger along the books, most of which she appeared to have read, giving Davy a whispered commentary on their contents. He had no idea so many miracles had been going on for so long. The ancient Egyptians, Christians, Muslims, Jews, Buddhists and more, they all had their miracles down the ages.

Donna slipped bits of paper into the books where she

found references to raising the dead. 'Leave them there for reshelving when you're done.' She hesitated. Gazing at George with tragic eyes she said, 'It's not me, I love dogs, it's just that Mrs Proot's very strict. Library rules.' George, hearing trouble in her tone, raised a paw. 'Oh, how adorable, he's asking to stay.' She checked no one was in earshot. 'You know what, though, guide dogs are allowed by law. I don't suppose . . . ?'

The two of them considered George. 'I think he could be,' Davy said.

As Donna squeaked her cart away, they sat on the floor and Davy began working through the pile. The books were rich with drawings and paintings. He discarded one book after another with their visions, healing the sick and saints hovering above the ground. None of them were what he was looking for, though he wouldn't have been able to say exactly what that was. Sighing, he stood for a last scan of the shelf. *The Lost World of Celtic Belief and Tradition*. Donna had passed that one by.

He sat down with it on his lap. It was satisfyingly heavy with plenty of colour pictures. Six pages in, he stopped in disbelief. It was the painting. The very one that had appeared in *Renaissance Angels* and then not been there when he'd shown it to Mr Timm. The night-time forest scene with the warrior and the hound keeping watch over the dead man laid out on the rock.

'I didn't imagine it,' he said to George. Just as he remembered, the hound and the warrior stared out from the page directly at him. Their eyes followed him as he moved.

There was a paragraph below the painting. 'Listen to this, George.' Davy read aloud, feeling his heart quicken as he did. '*In Celtic belief, the soul made a three-day passage between the worlds of the living and the dead. During this time, the body was guarded to ensure the soul's safe arrival in the afterlife.* A three-day passage,' he whispered. Could *this* be it? Quashing his conscience, he took hold of the page and, with a cough to cover the noise, ripped it from the book.

Heading back to Miss Flint, a thought sent him to the front desk. He could test out his theory right away. The '*o*'s on the name badge of Mrs M. Proot, Head Librarian, had *not* been made into little smiling faces. Her frown deepened at the sight of Davy. 'Yes?' she said sharply.

He pointed to the table where, surrounded by open books, Miss Flint was vainly, and with rising irritation, trying to click the switch of the flickering reading lamp. 'Excuse me, can you see anyone at that table?' he said.

Mrs Proot looked. She pursed her lips. 'All I see is you wasting my time. When you're done, return the books for reshelving. No dogs allowed.' She stared pointedly at George.

'He's a guide dog,' Davy said.

Her gaze narrowed in suspicion. 'Hmph,' she said.

Could it really be? Could she not see Miss Flint? Donna was squeaking along the stacks with her cart. Davy hurried over and, again, pointed at Miss Flint. 'That table,' he said. 'Do you see a woman sitting there?'

Donna craned her neck, smiling. 'Nope. Plenty of seats. You find what you were after?'

'I think so.' Davy's voice was faint.

Donna patted George Bailey and went off down a row. She couldn't see Miss Flint either. *They couldn't see her.*

Miss Flint was engrossed in her reading. She barely glanced up as he approached, saying, 'Do you know about quantum physics? Most extraordinary.'

'The librarian can't see you.' Davy didn't look at her as he took his bag from the back of the chair.

'There's this one experiment,' she said, reading, 'they shone light through slits and I just wonder –'

'She can't see you,' Davy said again.

'She ought to get her eyes checked.' Miss Flint looked

up and saw his face. 'Good grief, Mr David, what's wrong?'

He walked towards the exit. He had to get away. George followed anxiously.

'Wait,' she called. 'Where are you going? Mr David, get back here! Come back!'

Miss Flint couldn't be seen. But Davy could see her. And so could George.

Was she a ghost? Dead? Or maybe . . . not quite? *A three-day passage of the soul.* Maybe somewhere between alive and dead. The forest painting, appearing and disappearing in that strange way. Surely that couldn't be a coincidence. He couldn't think. He had to be alone and think. Her sunken weakness last night. The shallow gasps of her breath. Was it possible? *Could* she be dead?

Davy hurried down the block with George. As they turned the corner, he stifled a cry.

Miss Flint stood there.

'What possessed you?' she said. 'Running off like that? Goodness, you're pale. Are you all right? Mr David? Are you ill?'

'At the library,' he whispered. 'They couldn't see you.'

'You're developing a tendency to repeat yourself. And to whisper. Speak up.'

'I asked, they said no. The waitress at breakfast. She wasn't ignoring you. She couldn't see you. The man at the jukebox. He couldn't either.'

His heart thundered in his chest. With shivers chasing over his skin, Davy began to circle her slowly. Miss Flint's puzzled gaze followed him around. She appeared to be solid. He knew she *felt* solid. His hands had brushed her in passing throughout the day.

'Just now,' he said. 'You were blowing the pages. You couldn't turn them, could you?'

'Nonsense,' she said, 'I simply –'

'And the lamp. You couldn't work it, could you? Just like you couldn't work the switches in the police car. They shorted out, remember? I wonder why?'

Then, greatly daring, very gently, Davy reached out and felt her shoulder blades. One, then the other. Through her tweed jacket, he could feel how thin she was, the delicacy of her bones.

'What are you doing?' she said, uneasily.

'No wings,' he said to himself.

'Wings? I should think not. As if I were a bird or –'

'Or what?' he breathed. 'Or what?' He gazed at Miss Flint. Was it his imagination or was she looking even younger? Was her skin smoother? Were her eyes clearer?

'Why are you staring so? What's going on?'

'I don't know,' said Davy. 'Something strange.' He pulled the folded book page from his pocket. When she went to take it, she could not. He had to hold it for her to see. 'Read it,' he told her. 'Read it aloud.'

She sighed. Then she read, impatiently, '*In Celtic belief, the soul made a three-day passage between the worlds of the living and the dead. During this time, the body was guarded to ensure the soul's safe arrival in the afterlife.* A fanciful notion,' she said. 'So?'

'So, look at the picture,' Davy said.

Miss Flint stared at the forest painting. She frowned at Davy. 'You think I'm – dead?' She said the word delicately, as if trying it out.

'I think you might be . . . almost dead. Becoming dead.'

'*Becoming* dead? You're either dead or you're not.' But then, thought by thought, her eyes began to widen. 'Oh,' she said. 'Last night. Did I . . . pass in my sleep?'

'I think so.'

'But I can see myself in the mirror. And you can see me. You and George.'

He took her hand. It felt as fragile as a baby sparrow. The skin was dry and tissue-thin. 'I can feel you,' he said. She touched George's head and the dog looked up at her. 'George too. But no one else, Miss Flint. Just us.'

'Why?' she said.

Davy shrugged, helpless. 'I don't know.' He held the book page in front of her again.

She read silently once more. Then she raised her eyes to his. 'Let me understand this,' she said slowly. 'You believe that your purpose is to escort my soul to its embarkation point to the great beyond. A boy of thirteen and a stray dog.'

'I don't know,' said Davy. 'Maybe. Yes. I think so.'

'That's completely ridiculous,' said Miss Flint.

'Well, you explain it,' Davy said. He and George were following Miss Flint down the street. They kept a little distance to allow for her erratic pacing and doubling back.

'I can't!' she cried.

Miss Flint was in state of high agitation, so much so that the street lights in her vicinity were flashing. Davy suddenly understood. The flickering lights in the diner, the toaster and jukebox, the police radio and siren, the library reading light, they were all down to her. She must be giving off some kind of electrical interference.

'But I'll tell you this, Mr David. There's a rational explanation for everything.'

The town was in full Christmas bustle. It appeared

far more prosperous than Brownvale. To the mournful accompaniment of a Salvation Army brass band, honest citizens and petty villains alike went about their business. Emptying pockets, diving in and out of shops, hurrying along hoping not to be hailed, having to stop to exchange greetings with friends and enemies.

Not one of them took the least bit of notice of Miss Flint. But Davy saw how they flowed around her, as if they sensed an invisible obstruction in their path.

Invisible to all, that is, but the dogs and cats. Like the boxer on a leash, who cowered as his puzzled owner dragged him past. Or the big Alsatian on his own, who skittered across the road to avoid her. And the slinking cat, who arched and hissed and ran away. It seemed that George was rare in not fearing her.

'And I'll tell you something else,' Miss Flint continued. 'I can get where I'm going without you. Escorts to the embarkation point, indeed. I've never heard such guff. You're fired. Both of you. Pardon me.' She spoke to a passing woman. 'Where might I hire a taxi?'

The woman, not seeing her, made no reply and carried on.

Davy sat on a bench with George. Surreptitiously, he counted the money Miss Flint had given him. Half his wages in advance, more money than he'd ever dreamed of having. She'd fired him. He was under no obligation. He could take George and find some other place to call home, with a movie house and a library. Plenty of people moved from place to place. Maybe the city, they could go there and find Mr Timm. So long as Davy could still make his pictures.

He looked up. Miss Flint's attempts to stop someone, to get anyone to see her were becoming ever more frantic. Her reaching hands went unfelt. Her beseeching voice went unheard. Though the explanation for her predicament was beyond him, one thing was clear. She really was invisible to everyone but Davy and animals.

However, people were starting to notice her electrical agitations. The town's Christmas lights, drooping dimly along both sides of the street, had begun to flash madly, as currents chased up and down them. The animated window display of a nearby toy store was speeding up, going faster and faster, to comic effect. Passers-by crowded around to watch and laugh.

'I'm a self-determining human being. I'm an atheist,' cried Miss Flint. 'When we die, we're gone and that's it. We do not run around looking for taxis. And by the way, if I'm dead, where's my body?'

'Your body.' Davy had completely forgotten. 'We must have left it in your room. Do you need it?'

A man who'd stopped to light a cigarette gave him a peculiar look and hurried off.

'It's not a suit of clothes.' Miss Flint suddenly stopped. 'The New Inn,' she said. 'There was something – no, it's gone. I'll tell you what, Mr David, I'm beginning to think that *you're* the problem.' She pointed at him accusingly. 'Everything was fine till you came along. I had a schedule, a plan. You probably drove us off the road and I'm in a coma, dreaming all of this. Or wait – yes, that's it. Quantum physics! We're stuck in a quantum anomaly!' She pronounced it with conviction, her eyes blazing.

'What's that?' said Davy.

She threw up her hands. 'How should I know? No one understands quantum physics!'

She stood there, surrounded by the light storm she was causing, that she was charging ever higher with her frustration. Cars were stopping, people were coming out of shops.

'Miss Flint,' Davy said. 'Please. Just look around you.'

She did. She looked in wide-eyed wonder, turning this way and that. Davy saw the moment she understood she was the cause. He watched her face change. He saw the fright that seized her.

At that moment, a bus pulled up to a stop nearby. The door opened, passengers got off and a few began to get on. Miss Flint ran and climbed aboard. Davy could see her pay her fare. But when the bus pulled away, there she stood. In the street, holding her change purse, looking lost. She looked lost and alone and afraid.

And Davy realized. He suddenly knew. 'She can't leave,' he said. 'She can't go anywhere, not without us. You and me, George. I don't know why, but we're the only ones who can get her where she needs to go.'

Another bus was coming along the street. Miss Flint cried, 'That's our direction.' Davy didn't hesitate. He scooped up the briefcase, and George, and ran. When she got on, they were behind her. Miss Flint spoke to the driver, 'End of the line, for myself and the boy. How much?'

The bus abruptly cut out. The driver frowned, turning the key, flicking switches. But the bus played dead.

'You see? It's you,' Davy told her. 'We can't get out of here if you don't calm down.'

The driver glared at him. 'Mind your sass!'

Miss Flint took a deep breath. Then another. The bus started itself up again.

Shaking his head, perplexed, the driver said, 'OK, bub, where to?'

'End of the line,' said Davy.

The driver wheezed the doors shut and pulled away from the stop. They lurched their way down the aisle and sat on the long bench seat at the very back. Davy put George on his lap so he could look out. 'You can't get anywhere without us,' said Davy.

Miss Flint stared blankly. 'He can't see me. No one can.'

'We have three days to get you to your place of . . .' Davy couldn't remember the word.

'Embarkation,' she said.

'That's your house,' he said. 'At least, I think it is.'

He stared out the window. They'd cleared town and were on the open road. Oil derricks were scattered across the cracked earth. Their pump arms rose and fell, rose and fell. George's warm body was a reassuring weight on Davy's knee.

Miss Flint couldn't leave the world without his help. Davy turned his head and gave her a wry smile. He, Davy David, who'd never been needed before, was needed now in the most amazing way. '*This* is why you hired me,' he said. 'It's why you waited for me to come back.'

'What's happening to me?' she whispered.

'Something wonderful,' he said. 'Don't be afraid.'

The day was advancing when the bus rolled into the depot. The first day of Miss Flint being dead. The first day of Davy's new paid job, of him and George shepherding her soul to – where exactly? To her old childhood home by the sea, yes. But what would happen when they got there?

Davy had been pondering that during the several hours they'd been twisting through the countryside. And during the rest stop, when the driver had a smoke and some of the passengers bought barley coffee from a woman who'd pitched her tent where the bus pulled off. Riding on a bus, having money in his pocket to buy coffee should he wish to – these things were new to Davy. As was the fact that people acknowledged him, with a smile or nod or a few words while they stooped to fuss over George. Dogs, he was discovering, were a great leveller. And George was a friendly kind of dog.

Miss Flint stayed on board. He didn't want to

leave her, he was nervous she might disappear. But she reminded him that George needed a break and agreed to sit by the window so Davy could keep an eye on her.

Otherwise, she was inclined to silence and he let her be. She had to work out how she felt about becoming dead. Davy had his own thoughts about the world and its whys and wherefores. His ideas weren't hidebound, he always adjusted as he went along.

He wondered if this kind of thing went on all the time. Whether the world was full of people becoming dead. Sitting in libraries and cafes and walking the streets, desperate for the living to see them, to hear them, to help them on their way. If that was the case, he might have had an inkling before. Surely someone would have mentioned it. Still, it was hardly a subject for casual conversation. Donna from the library, who'd been so helpful, she'd be good to talk to. He didn't think she would be surprised if he were to tell her.

'Why am I getting younger?' said Miss Flint.

'I don't know,' Davy said. 'I just don't know.'

He took the folded page from his jacket several times to study the painting. The warrior and his great hound were the subjects, not the body laid out on the rock. The only light fell upon their faces, all else was shadowed to a greater or lesser extent. It was their eyes, their following eyes, which gave the power to the piece. He tried to read what they seemed to want to tell him. They were unafraid. With the darkness of the forest all around, concealing any number of unknown dangers, they remained steadfast. They knew their duty. Maybe that was it.

He stared at Miss Flint when she wasn't looking. His fingers itched to draw her new face. 'Do you have any paper in your briefcase?'

She nodded and waved a hand for him to help himself. As Davy clicked the case open, he suddenly recalled the bottle of pills, still in his pocket. She wouldn't be needing them now. He tried to sneak the bottle back into the case but she saw. She raised a questioning eyebrow.

'I thought . . . maybe I could talk you out of taking them,' he said.

There was a whole pad of writing paper. Davy took two sheets and filled them with tiny sketches of her face.

When the bus drew into the depot at the end of the line, they were the only three passengers left. Huffing a relieved breath, the driver gathered his coat and bag. 'Last stop! You and the pooch, off off off,' he called to Davy.

The depot was a tin building among an isolated

clutch of sagging warehouses and workshops. Half a dozen buses were parked inside. As they rolled into the last available space, the only person there, the woman in the tiny dispatch office, was putting on her coat.

'Hup hup!' The driver was clearly in a hurry.

As they got off, Miss Flint, forgetting she couldn't be heard, said to him, 'We're going west. When's the next bus?'

The office woman had turned off the lights and was locking the door. She'd been just about to pin a police poster on to the bulletin board, but now it would have to wait until after the holidays.

The driver called to her, 'Looking like a rose, Violet.'

Violet waggled flirtatious fingers at him, mincing along in her high heels, bulging and jiggling in her too-tight skirt and flowered blouse.

'She schedules all the shifts, so I keep her sweet,' the driver told Davy. 'Cigarettes. Perfume. A little brandy.'

With some difficulty, Violet hoicked herself on to a bicycle. Hanging her purse on the handlebars, she pedalled off unsteadily down the road, calling, 'See you later, Bert! Save me a dance!'

Bert clutched at his heart, watching her go. Davy repeated Miss Flint's question.

'No more buses tonight. You picked the wrong

day to travel. We're knocking off early, it's the depot Christmas party tonight.' Bert winked. 'Don't tell the boss. Wherever you're going, you'll get there quicker walking.'

While they talked, he'd been turning off the main lights and shooing them out. He began to pull the doors to.

'Knocking off early!' said Miss Flint. 'This is just the kind of thing we have to put up with nowadays. Don't tell the boss, indeed. The man's dishonest. I've a good mind to write a – We need to buy a car,' she said suddenly.

'A car?' said Davy.

'Of course. It's obvious. I should have thought of it before. Ask him where we can find the nearest car dealership.'

Davy was annoyed he hadn't thought of a car himself. She had plenty of money in the briefcase, he'd seen it there. He ran to help Bert pull the doors to. 'I need to buy a car,' he said.

Bert locked up with a key from a crowded ring dangling from his belt. 'A car? Sure you do. I've heard about you eccentric millionaires, you like to ride the bus disguised as twelve-year-olds.' Chuckling at his fancy, he walked over to a brown van with its side caved in.

Davy, Miss Flint and George followed him. 'No really, it's for a friend,' said Davy.

Davy was about to open the briefcase when Miss Flint hissed, 'Don't let him see! And don't call him sir, he's not a sir.'

Davy pulled her aside. 'Maybe not, but he's the kind of guy who knows people. Didn't you hear him? Cigarettes? Perfume?'

'You mean a dealer in stolen goods.'

'We need a car. We can't be fussy,' he said.

Bert opened the driver's door with a well-aimed kick and a heavy thump. As the door sprang open, six cartons of cigarettes tumbled out, with wrappers marked *Import Duty Due*. 'I uh . . . found them in an alley,' he said.

Miss Flint crossed her arms and gave Davy one of her lemon looks.

'Sir, I have money,' Davy said. He took the roll from his pocket, his half-wages in advance, secured with a red rubber band.

The sight of the money seemed to galvanize Bert. 'I might know someone,' he said. He leaped to his feet, hastily bundling the cartons back into the van, and opened the passenger door with another hefty kick. 'Young man, your chariot awaits.'

The van belched off in a greasy cloud of black market

diesel, with the three of them plus George wedged in by boxes of illegal cigarettes and perfume and crates of contraband French brandy.

Miss Flint's dark look predicted murder and worse. 'We'll be in shallow graves by sunset, you mark my words,' she said to Davy, forgetting she was already dead.

Back at the depot, the police poster sat on Violet's desk. It seemed that the barman from the New Inn had given a good description to the police sketch artist. For the boy staring out from the poster was clearly, recognizably, Davy.

Contrary to Miss Flint's predictions, they'd not been murdered. But they had been fleeced. Chewing on a toothpick, Bert's friend Vic sized up Davy, not bothering to hide his glee at being handed such a turnip. With a flurry of winks and nudges to Bert, he showed Davy the vehicle on offer. It was an ancient motorbike with a rusted sidecar.

Miss Flint made things worse by badgering him to make a deal. 'Offer him half. Tell him he's lucky to get anything for it, tell him you'll walk away. Go on, speak up.'

But as Davy opened his mouth, Vic pounced. 'The

price is the price. I don't negotiate, I don't discuss. Take it or leave it, sonny boy.'

'And to be waved off with handfuls of your own money, well!' Miss Flint's voice scathed Davy from the sidecar as he parped the motorbike down the drive. She'd complained non-stop as she climbed in with George. 'Handfuls of it, mind. Merry Christmas, indeed! I'll Merry Christmas them.'

George knew the kind of villains they were dealing with, she said. The dog had taken an instant dislike to Vic. He'd growled throughout the humiliatingly brief transaction and barked at him as Davy counted the money into his hand.

'I'll take it straight to the nuns for the orphans,' Vic smirked. 'It kills me to let her go, she's a sweetheart, runs like a dream.' He tapped the fuel dial. 'And I'm throwing in a full tank of gas, because I'm a sweetheart too and it's the season of joy.'

It was early evening and dark when they drove off. The single headlamp wavered a dim path ahead. Run on a dynamo, the uncertain hammer of the engine produced a timid, wavering light.

Davy got on with getting to grips with driving while Miss Flint carried on complaining. Luckily the rattle of the bike meant he couldn't hear her. He saw her fling her arm left and made the turn just in time.

West, they had to keep on heading west. He'd get Miss Flint to her house, come what may. The business of gathering souls wouldn't wait for latecomers, Davy felt certain of that. He'd got them transport. It wasn't princely, it was a wreck and they'd been cheated, but they were on the move and that was all that mattered.

Bert the bus driver sat alone at a corner table. He brooded into his beer, plotting various revenges on Vic for cutting him short on the motorbike deal.

The depot Christmas party was a noisy riot of revellers shouting over the deafening blast of recorded music. Violet was leading a conga line of drivers and mechanics around the Lodge. As they passed Bert's table, she broke off to a chorus of dismay.

'Bliss,' she said, easing off her shoes. 'Why so gloomy, Bert? You didn't unload something on the kid? And don't give me that look, I know you.'

As he complained about Vic, she began to frown. 'What would you say he looked like, that boy?'

'Normal. Nothing special.' Bert shrugged. 'Brown hair, medium height. Kind of starey eyes. He talked to himself, that's the only thing. Not to the dog, to the air.' He waggled his fingers spookily.

'Talking to himself,' breathed Violet. 'The sign of a

guilty conscience.' She hurried her shoes back on. 'He's wanted by the police, Bert. I saw. They sent a poster.'

Bert's eyes popped in alarm. 'No, Vi, no police, please. It's my busy time of year. Hey, a bottle of brandy for your mother. No charge.'

Violet stood, head high, the very model of justice. 'You may not have a conscience, Bert, but *I* do.' She swished through the swing doors to the entrance lobby where there was a pay phone. She bounced back five minutes later. Seating herself back down with a virtuous shimmy, she said, 'They're sending someone over right away.'

Sometime around midnight, the motorbike began to cough. Miss Flint suggested they might be low on gas. The fuel dial indicated full but when Davy tapped it, the arrow sank to empty. They were passing some woods. He rolled them off the road into the trees. The bike sputtered to silence.

'I expect that villain we bought it from tampered with the gauge,' said Miss Flint. She shooed George out and clambered from the sidecar. She was forced to fold and unfold her legs, like a stork. From being pretty much bent in half when she was ancient, Miss Flint's back had straightened and it turned out she was fairly tall. 'This really is the most inconvenient vehicle,' she said.

Davy got off the bike, saying, 'How come you can't just walk through things? Like in *The Ghost and Mrs Muir*?'

'It may come as a surprise to you, Mr David, but the movies are not a reliable guide to the laws of physics,' she said.

As she turned to face him, Davy took a step back.

Miss Flint was now much younger than sixty. By the pale light of the moon, he could see her hair was no longer streaked with grey. It was long and thick and, so far as he could tell, golden in colour. The skin of her face was smooth. Her figure was trim. Around her eyes, on her forehead, there were a few lines but that was it.

'What is it?' she said.

Davy swallowed hard. 'It's happened again,' he whispered. He quickly tipped the left-hand mirror so she could see.

Miss Flint went very still. She touched her mirror image with a tentative finger. Slowly, wonderingly, she felt her face and hair. She looked down at her body, her legs and her feet.

'Is this the laws of physics?' said Davy.

'I don't know.'

'How old are you now?'

'I'm not sure. It was so long ago I knew myself like this. Forty, maybe a bit less.'

'Will it keep happening? Will you go on getting younger? Where will it stop?'

'*You* stop!' she cried. 'No more questions. I don't know. How can I know?' She went walking off among the trees, hugging her arms around her waist.

Davy kept an eye on her as he fiddled with the fuel gauge. He saw her stoop to pick up a fallen pine cone and bow her head for a long moment as she realized she could not. It seemed like prying for him to watch, so he looked away.

George snuffled about the ground, nosing up the needles. He'd had a meat patty at the cafe that morning and, on Miss Flint's advice, a bowl of water. Davy wondered if he needed to eat more than once a day. And he realized, with a pleasant shock, that George was *his* dog. 'I'll have to get you a collar,' he said.

The fuel arrow had settled firmly on empty. Davy gave up and took in his surroundings. He'd never been in a wood before. Most of the trees in Brownvale had been killed by drought. There'd been his graveyard yews, of course, but they were gone now.

Then, to his astonishment, he saw Miss Flint sitting in a tree. Perched comfortably on a branch, she smiled down at him, calm as could be.

'How did you get up there?' he said.

'I don't know.' Miss Flint frowned. 'I was just remembering how I used to love to tree-climb and how long it had been and thinking this one would be a cinch and then I just . . . found myself here.'

Davy ran to climb one too, while George barked at him from below. They sat on their respective branches, legs dangling.

'Deciduous.' She was examining a dry leaf still clinging to its twig. '*Acer campestre*, field maple.'

'I never climbed a tree till now,' Davy said.

'Miss Elizabeth Flint was far too grim to climb trees. Lizzie Flint used to. But she hasn't been seen for many years.'

'Do you think we'll see her soon? Sorry, that was a question.'

'Never mind.' Miss Flint sighed. 'If I carry on like this, it's a certainty we'll see her.'

'Do you think there's a scientific explanation?'

'There must be. I want to *know*. My fleshly being no longer exists, so I'm not made of ordinary matter. Am I anti-matter?' She shook her head. 'I'm not even sure what that means. It would take greater minds than yours, mine and George's to work it out. And I'm sorry, that was shocking grammar, but I don't care.'

'Don't you . . .' Davy stopped.

'Go on.'

'It's just, if I was you, I wouldn't care about what or how. I'd want to know *why*. That's what I'd ask myself. Why.'

The night was clear of clouds. The stars dazzled. 'That's Cassiopeia, that W there,' Davy said. 'You see? The daddy-long-legs, that's Andromeda. And there's Perseus, just above. The one kind of like a bird. See its wings?' Davy might never have been inside a classroom but he'd gleaned bits of knowledge from library books. Miss Flint seemed surprised that he knew so many constellations.

'I always meant to learn my way around the night sky,' she said. He pointed out one or two of the lesser known ones and she repeated their names. 'If I happen to find myself up in the stardust, I'll blink down at you,' she said. After a moment, she began humming, then singing, quietly, '*You do something to me. Something that simply mystifies me . . .* I used to like dancing,' she said.

It was the way she said it. Davy just knew. 'Did you have . . . someone? A boyfriend?'

'I was engaged to be married once.' She went on quickly, 'It was so long ago, I've almost forgotten. And it's a long time since I heard this song.'

'Heard it?' Davy listened. He could just make out the faint sound of music. 'Hey, I can hear it too.' He swarmed down the tree to the ground. 'Whoever it is might have some gas. Let's go see.'

George ran on ahead of them. They heard voices cry out at his arrival.

It was a travellers' camp, makeshift and shabby. A small group – two white-haired elderly men, an older woman and a teenage girl – were gathered around a campfire. They seemed friendly enough, encouraging their two dogs and George to sniff and make acquaintance. The music came from a wind-up radio, pulling in the hissing signal of a dance music programme.

Davy hesitated, hidden in the trees. They hadn't spotted him. His instinct was to hang back out of sight. It was his Brownvale way of keeping to the edges. But he had to act differently now, he told himself. He had to get Miss Flint to her house – and to do that he needed gas for the bike.

'If you act confident, others believe you are and you'll believe it too,' Miss Flint whispered. He looked at her, irritated. 'Or so I've heard,' she said.

Slowly Davy emerged from his tree cover. Miss Flint followed, unseen, behind him.

The travellers stood when they saw him. One of the men called out, 'We have no money, friend. We are peaceful people.'

Davy held up his hands to show he meant no harm. 'I'm alone. No one else, just me.'

At that, they broke into smiles and welcomed him with every indication of pleasure. The teenage girl was named Arden. She introduced the three elderlies with her as Auntie Lou, Cyril and Otto. Otto's kind eyes twinkled as he shook Davy's hand. He spoke with a heavy accent of some kind. Both he and the jovial Auntie Lou were cordial. Cyril seemed in a world of his own, apparently conversing with the singer on the radio.

Arden made drinking motions. 'Too much juice,' she told Davy. 'He lost his wife and kids to the flu. Drank so much his brain went spongy.'

Arden was older than Davy, around sixteen, he thought. She had dead black, short-cropped hair, dark slashes of brow and thick lashes. Her pale eyes were big in her thin face. Were they green? Or grey? Davy couldn't tell in the night. She made him feel shy. He couldn't find the nerve to look at her directly.

They did have gas they could sell him. Otto climbed into the cabin on the back of their old truck and emerged with an almost full jerrycan. He decanted half into a battered plastic container. Davy was careful to turn away while he pulled the money from his roll of cash. A roll that was getting leaner all the time.

Miss Flint hovered in frowning suspicion while Otto filled the bottle. He poured slowly and didn't stint them a drop. 'Now there's an honest man,' she said approvingly.

Davy was used to being alone with her, so didn't think and said, 'Now you owe me for the motorbike *and* the gas.'

'Hmm?' said Otto.

'Just talking aloud,' he had to say.

Miss Flint said, 'Pay yourself from the briefcase. Take what you want.'

She went and sat by the fire, where Arden and Auntie Lou argued good-naturedly as they tended the potatoes baking in the embers. 'It did *not* happen that way,' Arden was saying. 'Ma told me that story dozens of times.' She looked up at the sky. 'Tell her, Ma!' she said.

'Everyone has their own version of the past.' Miss Flint and Auntie Lou spoke at the same time.

Otto was speaking to him. 'What's that?' said Davy.

'I was just saying, you are not the only one. All of us here, we talk to ourselves. Some of us talk to the air. Me, I have been so long alive, I must talk to the dead. For no one else knows me or my life so well.'

The potatoes were ready. They invited Davy and George to join them. 'Auntie Lou,' said Arden. 'We could have our Christmas now. Tonight, with Davy.'

'The boy might be on his way to family,' she said.

'No,' said Davy. He held up the container of petrol, looking at Miss Flint. 'But I should get going.'

'A seasonal feast under the stars. Surely we have a little time to spare.' Miss Flint wasn't the wistful type, but she looked as if she wouldn't mind staying.

'I could stop a while, I guess,' Davy said.

Arden put candle stubs into glass jars and lit them. Davy shinned up nearby trees for her to hand them up and he placed them carefully in the crooks of the branches. They made bright points of light in the darkness.

'Like stars,' said Davy.

'That's what I call fine,' said Arden. 'A whole grove of Christmas trees, not just one.'

No king's banquet could have bettered that meal of baked potato with slices of sausage sizzled in a cast iron pan. The sausage was German because of Otto. They'd been saving it for Christmas with great anticipation, Otto explaining at length how and where he'd managed to procure it.

'We come empty-handed to the feast,' said Miss Flint.

With some shame, Davy remembered how he'd wolfed down his large breakfast that morning. He wished he had it again to share with them. Arden had to help Cyril to eat, cutting up his food and guiding the fork to his mouth. The dogs enjoyed the same meal as the humans, George included.

Davy thought they must be family, the way they interrupted and finished each other's sentences. But only Auntie Lou and Arden were related. They'd all been neighbours, wherever they came from that was so bad they had to pick up and leave. They'd been on the road for over two years, making stops for Otto to sharpen knives and scissors with his whetstone, which sustained them. He was teaching Arden his trade.

Miss Flint sat among them, unseen and unheard, except by Davy and George. No one else to glance her way, no one to include her. She watched and listened intently, with a kind of hunger, Davy thought. As for him, not used to such fellowship, he stayed largely silent. He felt like an eavesdropper in plain sight, though Auntie Lou and Otto tried to draw him out.

Once they'd finished eating and toasted Christmas with cups of watered-down beer, Otto stood and flung his arms wide to the twinkling trees. 'I will sing their special song.' Then he sang in German in his hoarse voice, a song called 'O Tannenbaum'.

While Otto sang, Miss Flint said to Davy, 'I can't remember when I had a nicer evening. Would you do something?'

'What?' he whispered.

'Make them one of your pictures.'

'I don't have my brooms.'

'You don't need them.'

'I'll be right back,' Davy told Arden.

He ran to the motorbike with George, unlocked the storage compartment of the sidecar and took out his bag, heavy with the weight of *Renaissance Angels*. On his way back to the campsite, he collected a branch of fir and various twigs. Otto was still singing. His melodious voice rang through the woods.

Davy sat beside Miss Flint and fluttered through the book, deciding which painting to make. 'That one,' said Miss Flint. She'd chosen the Tolmeo, *Angels Among the Magi*.

'I just did that one yesterday morning,' he whispered.

'Then you ought to be good at it,' said Miss Flint.

Otto finished his song and, prodded by Miss Flint, Davy stood up. His stomach was tight, his ears hot. He'd never swept in front of anyone before. 'I'd like to make a picture, to say thank you.'

'You're an artist,' Arden said, with some surprise.

Using the fir bough, he quickly smoothed a patch of earth, then got to work with the twigs. Once he had the feel of the ground and set up a rhythm, he forgot all about them being there. Miss Flint kept George sitting beside her. When Davy was done, they all crowded around and exclaimed in admiration.

Otto said, 'I thought I would have to wait to see angels, but here they are right at my feet.'

Though the picture was just as it ought to be, just as he'd done before, Davy wasn't satisfied. He took a swipe at it with his boot.

There was a burst of protest. Arden grabbed his arm, 'Hey, don't! It's amazing,' she said.

'It's just copying.' Davy looked at Miss Flint. 'A true artist makes his own pictures,' he said.

The radio had been playing quietly in the background. Cyril turned it up and began to dance, holding out his arms as if he had a partner. Davy recognized the song from the first few notes. It was one that Fred Astaire sang in *Top Hat*.

'Oh, I love this one!' Auntie Lou exclaimed. Springing to her feet, she held out her arms to Otto, singing, '*Heaven, I'm in heaven* . . . Come on, Otto! Let's us old folk show the youngsters how it's done.'

They began to dance together around the clearing. '*When we're out together dancing cheek to cheek,*' sang Otto.

Miss Flint said to Davy, 'Don't sit there moping, you gave them pleasure. You've got a pretty girl right beside you. Ask her to dance.'

He shook his head. 'I don't know how,' he whispered.

'I'll coach you, talk you through the steps. Don't be a bumpkin,' she said. 'Go on. Ask the girl nicely, *Would you care to dance?*'

'Would you care to dance?' Davy mumbled.

'Sure,' said Arden.

Miss Flint stood beside him. 'The gentleman always leads. Right arm around your lady's back. Left hand holding hers. This is a foxtrot. Your right foot steps forward first, then your left. Slow slow, step, quick quick, that's the rhythm. Ready? Here we go.'

She danced next to him and he copied her. After a couple of early stumbles, he caught the rhythm.

His hands were clammy as he held Arden at a careful distance.

'Good grief, she won't break. Hold her closer,' said Miss Flint.

'Stop bossing me!'

'What?' said Arden.

'Sorry. Talking to myself again,' said Davy.

'You're doing fine.' She smiled. 'You're quite the Fred Astaire.'

Davy, busy concentrating on his feet, said, 'I've seen him dance. At the movies.'

'*Flying Down to Rio*. That's Auntie Lou's favourite.'

'*Top Hat*.' Miss Flint and Davy said it together.

'No contest,' Davy added.

Arden looked at him curiously. Davy realized Miss Flint had stopped dancing beside him. Now he was dancing on his own.

The song finished and, as another began, they switched partners. Davy went with Auntie Lou and Arden danced with Otto. Miss Flint watched them with a look of such aching regret that Davy truly wished he hadn't seen it.

Then Cyril did something unexpected. He bowed to an imagined lady with old-fashioned courtesy and it happened that he bowed in front of Miss Flint. He held out his hand. 'Would you care to dance, my dear?' he said to the air.

'Thank you, I'd love to,' Miss Flint replied.

He made a circle of his arms and she slipped inside them. Then Cyril began to dance with his imaginary partner and Miss Flint began to dance with Cyril. She was graceful and elegant, turning and gliding, and she almost, very nearly, looked happy.

Two songs later, Davy found himself yawning. Auntie Lou said, 'That's enough for me.' Otto gave up too. Davy's eyes were so gritty he couldn't keep them open. Auntie Lou made him comfortable with a blanket on the ground and George came to curl up beside him.

The last thing Davy saw before slipping off sleep was Miss Flint and Cyril and Arden. The three of them, dancing together in the night-time woods, with stars twinkling among the branches of the trees.

When Davy woke, it was the darker side of dawn. George's warm little body curled into his side. Arden was rolled in a sleeping bag by the cold fire. One hand rested on *Renaissance Angels*, which was laid beside her. She must have been looking at it after Davy fell asleep.

Miss Flint. Where was she? A sudden fear shot Davy to his feet. In the rush, George got scrambled up from his sleep on to all fours, much to his surprise and annoyance.

No. Miss Flint was there. She hadn't disappeared while Davy slept. She lay a little way off, beneath the trees. Davy went over. Her eyes were closed. A flutter of night moths danced around her. She was some years younger than she had been last night, unrecognizable as the old woman he'd met two days before. He stared down at her. She was so peaceful, so still.

He stayed there, just watching her. Trying to memorize her every feature. She seemed paler to him as well as younger. Was it his imagination or was she less substantial than she'd been? Davy wondered what stuff she was made of. The moths seemed intent upon the air surrounding her, he could hear the soft flower-beat of their wings. He had a fancy they were weaving her into the dawnlight.

A whisper of a smile curved her lips, like she might be dreaming. Did the nearly dead sleep? Could they dream in the in-between? If so, what was she dreaming of? The sea? And he wondered if being dead was like a never-ending dream.

Davy sat on a fallen tree, taking the ripped book page from his pocket. In the greyish light, he examined it again. The warrior, his hound and the pale body they guarded. The woods in the painting were very like the woods around him. The difference was, they were alert, they were vigilant. *They* would never fall asleep and leave the soul of their charge unattended.

George, who after a stretch had gone to water a tree and sniff around, came over to Davy. 'We have to do better,' Davy told him.

There was no sign of the three elders or their two dogs, just Arden by the fire. Davy presumed they were sleeping in the cabin on the back of the truck.

Pre-dawn was his usual time to rise. Back in

Brownvale, it was when he made his angel pictures. He found the twigs he'd used last night and, silently, so as not to wake Arden or Miss Flint, he smoothed a circle of earth. He wrote *Merry Christmas. Thank you.* He took George's front paw, pressed a pawprint and wrote *George.* Beside his own handprint he wrote *Davy.*

'And me. Lizzie.' Miss Flint's whisper startled him. She was standing, watching him. He wrote *Lizzie,* thought for a moment, and drew some some wings.

He looked at Otto's old truck with its nearly bald tyres. He remembered how Auntie Lou's hand had hesitated before she cut the sausage, the whole thing, into generous pieces. It had probably been meant to last them some time. Davy took the roll of money from his pocket, removed the rubber band and laid the little stack below their names, weighting it down with a stone.

He crouched beside Arden, meaning to ease *Renaissance Angels* from under her hand. He paused.

The book had filled his life since he was nine, when the Home going bust had thrown him out into the world. Going to the library to study the paintings on its pages, committing details to memory, planning which painting he'd make, and where, had given purpose to his days. But the book and Brownvale and everyone there – Parson Fall, Mr Timm, Miss Shasta – it was all beginning to seem like a dream. And it felt to Davy that somehow, in some way, his real life had begun when he drove out of town with Miss Flint.

He didn't need the book any more. All its paintings were stored inside him. And it was time he tried to make his own pictures. He stood up.

'Are you certain?' said Miss Flint.

Davy nodded.

They crept away with George as Christmas Eve began to dawn.

He screwed the fuel cap back on, stowed the empty bottle in the sidecar's storage compartment, and checked the sky. 'West is that way,' he said, pointing.

Miss Flint had been pacing while he filled the tank, becoming more and more animated. He could almost see her winding up.

She said, 'In the last two days, I've hitchhiked, I've stolen turkeys and set them free. I took a police car without permission, bought a motorbike from a petty crook, and I – the woman formerly known as Miss Elizabeth Flint – last night, I danced in the moonlight in the woods.' She seized him by the arms, urgently. 'I've lived more being dead these few days than I have my last seventy years of being alive. You're thirteen and you understood right away. This thing that's happening to me – the what, the how – we can't know. They don't matter. You're right. It's the *why*. This.' She flung her arms wide. 'All of this, Davy, *this* is the why.'

He could tell there was more to come. He waited.

'His name is Robert Craig,' she said. 'He works, at least he worked, in a bank. I heard he married and had a daughter. It's not far out of our way.'

Davy was shaking his head even as she spoke. 'There's no time. I have to get you to the house. We still have a way to go.'

'I've been given the most extraordinary gift,' Miss Flint said. 'I don't deserve it, but I know what I have to do. And I can't do it without you and George.'

'He might not live there anymore. He could be dead – you are,' said Davy. 'What if we go looking for him and you get stuck somewhere as a ghost forever? It could happen. You don't know, we just don't know.'

Miss Flint was quiet for a moment, the blaze of certainty fading from her face. Then she said, 'Of course, Mr David. I'm sure you're right. Let's just get to where we have to be as soon as possible.'

He should have known. She'd let him win the argument too easily. He should have stopped to buy a map instead of following her directions without question. The warrior in the forest would never have fallen for such a trick. Davy could just see him shaking his head in disbelief.

Cruising the motorbike slowly so they could count the numbers on the houses, he glanced at Miss Flint in the sidecar. Raising his voice over the noise of the engine, he said, 'If this all goes wrong, it won't be my fault, so don't even think about haunting me.'

'I heard you the first twenty times,' she said. 'I make no apology, so don't expect one.'

There were two long rows of houses joined together, running along both sides of the street. Its pavements were surprisingly busy, with house doors opening and shutting. Adults ushered children along, calling for the laggers to catch up. The whole street, it seemed, was on the move, all headed for the same place, the corner building at the end of the block ahead. Neighbours greeted one another, exchanging a word or a wave. The loose chop of their bike caused heads to turn.

Davy consulted the torn-out page of a phone book. He didn't really need to look again, he knew the number. Nineteen. But he was feeling unexpectedly jumpy about this detour and it gave him something to do. Mentally he added *Vandalizing a phone book in a public box* to their ever-growing list of crimes. Judging from the book's plucked state, it was a common misdemeanour.

'I'm nervous,' said Miss Flint. 'Who would ever think you could be nervous when you're almost dead? I hope you're taking notes, Mr David. You ought to write a book afterwards. It would have to be fiction, of course. No one would credit this as fact.'

'It's just there, up on the right.'

The moment Davy finished speaking, the door of number nineteen opened and a tall, white-haired man emerged. Shutting the door behind him, he hurried down the block with everyone else. He wore a tail suit and bow tie, like Fred Astaire. He had a leather folder tucked underneath his arm. His step was strong. His back was straight. He strode along, exchanging greetings with those he passed.

'Is that him?' said Davy.

'I can't tell from behind.' Miss Flint was craning her neck. 'He did have good posture, he was in the army for a while.'

The man disappeared into the rear door of the building on the corner. As they came up, they saw it was marked *Stage Door*. The audience bustled in through the front in an excited hubbub. Davy nosed the bike crookedly into the kerb, killed the engine and hopped off.

He leaned into the sidecar, picking up George and the briefcase. Miss Flint had huddled herself into the corner. 'What's the matter?' he said.

'I was so certain,' she said. 'So sure I had to see him one last time. Now I'm here, I just don't know. What if it isn't him? What if it *is*? What do I do?'

'Don't ask me, this was your idea. We're doing the why, like you said.'

Miss Flint didn't budge.

'You won't find out sitting here,' said Davy.

She still didn't move.

'We'll see you inside,' he said. 'Come on, George.'

The theatre lobby was crowded and buzzing. Its worn carpet and patched paint and framed posters of past shows reminded Davy sharply of the Bellevue. It even smelt like it, of dampness and stale shoes and the dust of old dreamings. Maybe all theatres smelt the same.

A waistcoated usher began to ring a handbell, calling out, 'Take your seats! Three minutes, ladies and gents. Three minutes to curtain.'

Davy squirmed through to the box office and said to the woman behind the grille, 'Excuse me, ma'am, what's going on?'

'Annual Christmas show, dear,' she said. 'For Poor Relief.' She shook George's paw. 'Just the two of you?'

'Is, uh . . . Mr Robert Craig in the show?'

She threw up her hands, exclaiming with high drama, '*Is he in it?* the boy asks! Only every year for the past forty years. That's why they all come, dear. Mr Craig's our star turn.' Davy paid, telling her to keep the change. 'The poor thank you, dear, as do I. Dogs go free.' She pushed him a ticket. 'Enjoy the show.'

The lobby was rapidly emptying. The last few people rushed through the doors, but no Miss Flint. The usher took Davy's ticket, gave him a handbill and pointed him to the only free seat on the end of the last row. He slipped into it, settling George on his lap and the briefcase at his feet. As the lights dimmed, he glanced over the handbill, which was a running order for the show. There were ten acts in all, with Mr Robert Craig last to appear. He would sing a song called 'Silent Worship' by G. F. Handel.

A scratchy orchestra began to play from the pit in front of the stage, the red velvet curtain rattled up and the show began. In front of dog-eared panels painted with a jungle scene, a succession of performers entertained them. A pair of small girls dressed as fairies skipped about to general delight. A determined boy wheezed his accordion through a polka, the audience clapping along to encourage him. An elderly lady, warbling a folk song while plucking a harp, came to a puzzled halt halfway through, announced she'd forgotten the words and started all over again. A man wearing a fez performed comic magic tricks.

Davy didn't know what to expect, having never been to a theatre show before. They shouldn't be here, they should be on their way, but here he was so he might as well enjoy it. Of Miss Flint, however, there was no sign.

Outside, the beat officer paused by the motorbike. He walked around it, peered into the sidecar and wrote down the number plate. Then he went into Goessen's Drugs down the block to ask the boy serving there whether he had seen the driver.

The boy said he'd been swamped by folk at the last minute wanting cones of candy for the show at the old Rivoli and, Mr Goessen having gone to the show, he was on his own and had been that busy somebody could have parked a tank outside and he wouldn't have noticed.

The cop ordered a bromo for his indigestion and, while the boy mixed it, used the store's phone booth to call the station.

The curtain was dropped just before Robert Craig came on. Through the chatter of excitement Davy could hear sounds backstage, the rumble of things being moved about. The audience all seemed to know what was going on and welcomed the closed curtain as a thrilling build to the climax of the show. His neighbour, recognizing a stranger, told him how the stage was being cleared. He said how every year Mr Craig brought in a conductor specially for the occasion, a professional from a city orchestra, his fee paid for by Mr Craig. To Davy, it seemed a lot of fuss for one song by one old man.

Then, by some signal he must have missed, it all went quiet. The city conductor appeared in the orchestra pit and bowed to the audience. Davy was expecting applause, they'd clapped all the other acts from start to finish, but they were quiet. It was as if some spell had been cast, binding them to silence. After a moment, the curtain was raised again.

There stood Robert Craig. The man from number nineteen stood alone in a spotlight in the darkness on the empty stage. With his mane of white hair and a rose in his lapel, he was as fine an old man as ever was. Davy looked, but Miss Flint was still not there.

The conductor lifted his hands and the music began and Davy understood why he'd been brought from the city. He made that scratchy orchestra sigh like a breeze on a summer's day. Then Robert Craig began to sing and Davy was spellbound with the rest.

'Did you not hear My Lady
Go down the garden singing?
Blackbird and thrush were silent
To hear the alleys ringing.'

His voice was clear and high and beautiful. It was a young man's voice, fresh and full of hope. It was so entirely unexpected, so impossible, that the first sound of that voice brought tears to Davy's eyes. He couldn't help it. The tears just came, unbidden.

And, at last, Davy saw Miss Flint. He watched as she walked slowly up the middle aisle of the Rivoli. Her gaze was fixed on the singer as she moved towards the stage. She, too, had been enchanted.

'Though I am nothing to her
Though she must rarely look at me
And though I could never woo her
I love her till I die.'

She stopped just before the pit and stood there, pressing her hands to her heart, as if it hurt.

'But surely you see My Lady
Out in the garden there
Rivalling the glittering sunshine
With a glory of golden hair.'

The orchestra's last note faded to silence. Silence. Then the audience, as one, rose in a swell of cheering that raised the roof of the glad old Rivoli. Robert Craig bowed and bowed. Though they knew better than to ask for more – he'd not obliged them for twenty years – they called 'Encore!' He opened his hands as if to feel the fall of long-desired rain. But they must be satisfied with one song, as he had to be. For his voice was now rare as ancient glass.

Miss Flint stood in the aisle with her hands clasped to her heart. Robert Craig was smiling and smiling, slipping the rose from his lapel, touching it to his lips. He was smiling at *her*.

He could see her.

Davy scrambled on to his chair to get a better view. Miss Flint took a step as the old man leaned forward and tossed the rose. She reached for it – she reached but didn't catch it. Of course. She could not.

And Davy saw from his vantage point. He saw. The white-haired woman standing in the aisle behind Miss Flint, applauding. He saw that Robert Craig looked at her and not Miss Flint. He saw him smile at her, throw the rose to her. Davy saw her catch it.

'His wife,' said the man next to Davy. 'He always does that. Fifty years they've been married.'

And Davy saw Miss Flint's face as she turned, as she saw his wife. Davy saw the understanding and the regret and the pain come to her all at once.

And he thought that surely she was mistaken about the why. For it couldn't be right, how could it be meant for her heart to be broken just as she left the world?

*

The audience filed out, chattering, and Davy swam against the tide to the front row, where Miss Flint sat staring into space. In the pit, the orchestra packed away their instruments. He and George sat beside her. 'I knew we shouldn't have come,' he said. 'I wish we hadn't.'

Miss Flint turned her head to Davy. Tears trembled like a fall of stars upon her cheeks. 'I had to see him before I go. I had to know he's all right. That his life turned out well. That he's happy. And he is.'

'But you're crying,' Davy said.

'Yes. Yes, I am,' she replied. 'I'd die a hundred times over to feel this way.'

Davy didn't understand. But he tried to memorize how she looked, so he could draw her face later on. At last he said, 'We'd better go.'

As they stood, Davy saw the policeman. He'd stationed himself by the doors so he could see everyone who filed past. The moment Davy spotted him, he spotted Davy. He began to move towards them.

'Police. Come on,' Davy said.

They ran up the stairs at the side of the stage, dodging through a door into a corridor full of people. There were dressing rooms either side, overflowing with performers and well-wishers. Miss Flint's proximity set all the lights fizzing as Davy squeezed through with George in his arms.

Robert Craig said jovially, 'What's the hurry, young fellow?'

Miss Flint paused in front of him. She went on tiptoe. 'Goodbye, Robert.' She gently kissed him on the lips and his head jerked back, as if he'd had a shock.

The heavy-set policeman appeared at the door to the stage, wincing as he clutched at his side. 'Hurry,' said Davy.

They dashed out the stage door, over the road, on to the motorbike. Davy gunned it to life and they were gone.

The night had bedded in when the motorbike began to kick and judder. Then the engine cut out completely and they coasted to a halt. Davy knew they had enough fuel. He attempted to restart it, but the bike was dead.

'Don't waste your time, it's only good for scrap,' said Miss Flint. As George leaped from the hated sidecar, she climbed out nimbly and Davy stared.

She must have been shedding years by the hour as they travelled. She was in her twenties now, her skin blooming with freshness. Her hair gleamed. Her eyes glowed. She was lovely.

She could tell by his face that she'd changed again. Davy tipped the bike mirror and she took a long look at herself. 'Well, I'll be,' she said softly. 'Lizzie Flint. It's been a very long time since I saw you.'

Her buoyant spirit from earlier was gone though. Since seeing Robert Craig, she'd been silent with her thoughts.

There was a crossroads just ahead. From the storage compartment, Davy took her briefcase and his cloth bag, now empty but for his drugstore items. He gave the bike a disgusted kick in passing as they walked the few yards to take a view. They were on high ground. The land had been climbing gently the last mile or so before the bike gave up.

It was a lonely place. There were no lights of human habitation, near or distant. The sky was clear, with a bright round moon. The air was light and cool. What looked to Davy like flat grassland spread out in every direction, punctuated by clusters of low growing brush.

'They call this place The Grass,' Lizzie said.

The crossroads signpost sprouted a cluster of wooden fingers pointing in the four directions. Davy couldn't make out the place names and distances painted on them, they'd faded so badly. Lizzie came to take a look.

'Are we near?' Davy asked her.

'It's that way,' she replied, pointing. 'But across The Grass, it's only a few miles as the crow flies. The road takes the long way around.'

Davy glanced at the sky. 'There's the Pole Star. All we have to do is keep it on our right shoulder.'

'Let's wait,' she said. 'There'll surely be a car passing soon. We can get a lift.'

Chilled through from being on the bike, Davy stomped his feet and blew on his hands. He scooped up George and warmed himself by hugging the dog's strong little body. Lizzie walked a few paces along each road and back again.

The earth underfoot gave off a different feel than that of Brownvale. It seemed to have a restless, seeking energy. He could smell the winterkill of the stubby grass.

There was a worn rectangular stone fallen on its side. He went to sit on it with George and listen for any sound of a vehicle.

Lizzie stood with her arms crossed, looking around. 'My mother liked to walk here. I never did.'

Davy thought of the boy in the photograph. Had he come too? Had he liked walking here, he and their little dog? He hesitated, then asked her something that was on his mind. 'What do you think's happening to your body?'

'I imagine it's in cold store in some mortuary,' Lizzie said. 'They'll probably have to keep it there until after the holidays. The old tend to die around Christmas. Perhaps spring just seems too far away. Wherever it is, it's beginning to decay.'

'They buried my mother in Potter's Field back in Brownvale. Where will you go?' he said.

'Nowhere. Everywhere. Ashes to ashes. If my paperwork catches up with my body in time, they'll know to cremate me.' She sat down next to him.

'I planted a rose for her. I'd plant one for you,' Davy said.

'An apple tree.' She smiled. 'A tart apple. More fitting, don't you think?'

'Can I ask you something else?'

'You may,' she said.

He hesitated, then said, 'How does it feel?'

She didn't have to ask what he meant. She knew. 'Our atomic composition is mainly hydrogen, water,' she said. 'If you calculate by mass, we're made of oxygen, sixty-five per cent.' She turned her head to look at him. 'Either way, I'm evaporating. Thinning to the air, body and soul. I feel lighter and lighter all the time.'

'I better hang on to you, then.' Davy took her hand.

She was right. She was like a feather, insubstantial.

A slight uneasiness prowled in Davy's bones. It probably wasn't the place, more the time pressing on his mind. He tipped George from his lap and stood up. 'It's got to be midnight. We need to keep moving.'

'Crossing The Grass at night is just foolhardy,' she said. 'It's not safe. For you, I mean, not me. The ground's rough, you could easily fall.'

'We don't know how much time you have left.'

'You have to be prepared for the conditions. You need the right equipment, the right clothing. The weather here can be unpredictable.'

'It's grass. It's a clear night.'

'You'll need a walking stick. The conditions . . . What are you doing?'

He emptied the contents of the briefcase into his bag – her little painting, the photograph, the banded stacks of money – and slung it across his chest. 'Do you want that?' He indicated the briefcase. She shook her head.

He searched about and found a good-sized sturdy stick. He tested its strength, swiping it through the air. 'OK,' he said. 'I'm prepared for the conditions.'

He whistled for George. He took Lizzie by the hand. He led them out on to The Grass.

The air had been calm at the crossroads. Out on The Grass, it was blowing a strong westerly. The ground was rough and uneven, like she'd said, dipping and rising underfoot without warning. Davy used his stick as they went along. With no large landmarks to plot their path, it all looked much the same. It seemed endlessly open. He kept a careful watch on the Pole Star.

George played scout, running ahead and returning to them. They came upon a standing circle of stones, worked with symbols like the one they'd sat on at the crossroads. The wind was so loud in Davy's ears that he had to lean in close to hear Lizzie. Even though she was right next to him and he held her hand.

'They think this was a ritual landscape,' she said. 'Thousands of years ago. Ancient beliefs. Ceremonies. The whole place. The land, the sky, the spirit. All connected through the stones.'

It was a far cry from the preachings of Parson Fall.

'Like in a church?' said Davy.

Lizzie shook her head. 'Older. Wilder. Unknown.'

The wind buffeted them strongly. Davy soon found he was having to lean into it to make progress. He was unpleasantly aware of his body's flimsiness. He feared that Lizzie, with her terrible lightness, might blow away. He stopped to tuck himself closely in behind her. 'Let it push you against me,' he told her.

They moved forward step by step. His legs were having to dig in to keep them upright. He was thankful to have the stick for support. The wind was a constant whine in his ears. George was choosing to stay close to them.

The wind suddenly switched direction. It came howling at them from the right. With a shriek, Lizzie was thrown from the shelter of his body. Davy grabbed her hand just in time. Instinctively, he sheltered her in his arms. 'Put your arms around me,' he yelled.

As they stood there, the wind abruptly changed again. No longer howling, it seemed to prowl around them in a shivering, hissing circle. Shadows within it seemed to shift and stretch. The thought came to him that the wind had some kind of intent. No doubt Lizzie would call him ridiculous.

But George was growling. His hackles were up. His teeth were bared.

Davy's scalp prickled. 'What is it? I can't see anything.'

'Dogs have senses we don't. But I feel something.'

Davy nodded. So did he.

'Mother could be fanciful. She said something once. She said that The Grass holds dreams of ancient rituals and old beliefs. Land, sky and spirit. All connected.'

Davy said, 'It's you, halfway between – I think you've wakened it.'

He stared at her.

The wind began to circle faster, wailing higher. They could feel it closing in. George was snarling, lunging out. As if he were keeping something at bay.

'You can't leave from here,' Davy shouted. 'It's the wrong place.'

'Hold on to me,' cried Lizzie. 'Don't let me go.'

Davy felt his weakness. He was no warrior. No hero. He was just a boy. Yet here was George, a small dog, protecting them. Dashing boldly at the dark heart of the wind.

If you act confident, others believe you are and you'll believe it too.

Davy had had to be courageous, in his way. His life in Brownvale had demanded it. He had the steady-eyed warrior folded in his pocket. He had George. They would get Lizzie home, as he'd promised. Davy stood tall. 'Are you wearing a belt?' he shouted.

She nodded.

'Keep your arms around me.' He took his belt off, slipped it through his side belt-loop and fastened it around Lizzie's belt. Would it work? Could it? Lizzie's belt joined with his? He didn't know the rules governing her passage. He tugged at them. 'Can you feel that?'

Again she nodded.

He grabbed his stick that he'd dropped. Taking firm hold, raising it high, Davy walked forward, slashing at the wind. 'Out of the way! Clear the way,' he yelled fiercely.

He felt it give, just slightly, as he slashed. He felt himself clearing a narrow pathway for them to move through, as if the wind could bend like a wall of reeds. Lizzie clutched at his sleeve.

Then, without warning, a mist sucked up from the ground, and the wind became a whirling haze of white fog. They were enveloped, enclosed, moving blind. If he'd had the slightest doubt there was intent, that doubt was gone.

'Move aside!' he yelled, slashing.

The wind rushed at them. Davy lost his footing and the stick flew from his hand. George raced off barking, in pursuit to retrieve it.

'It's trying to take me!' Lizzie yelled.

He wrapped his arms around her. The wind turned them in circles, pushing as it staggered them in relentless progress to where it would. Davy was helpless to do anything but cling to Lizzie.

Then, suddenly, they were almost on top of George. He was muddy to the chest and had Davy's stick in his mouth. He was dragging it, running across their path to and fro, seemingly frantic.

'Give me that!' Davy yelled. He lunged, grabbing for the stick and George dodged off to the side. Davy's right boot went into wet sucking ground and stuck there.

'Bog!' shouted Lizzie. 'He was warning us!'

Davy bent, hauling on his boot with all his might. As it flew free, he fell over. Lizzie, joined by their belts, fell on top of him. George dropped the stick at his hand and Davy grabbed it.

Barking, running back and forth, George was urging them to follow him. Davy realized he'd keep them away from the boggy ground. On their feet again, they kept low, almost crouching, as Davy slashed a path through the howling, whirling fog.

He felt the ground beneath his feet begin to rise. George was leading them up to higher ground. Then a pile of slabbed stones loomed in front of them. They scrambled to press themselves against the rock.

And the wind quit. Abruptly. Just like that. And just like that, too, the fog was gone.

The only noise was Davy gasping for breath. The Grass rolled out serenely in the moonlight. He stared. Where had it gone? He looked at Lizzie, huddled next to him. Her eyes were wide.

'Are you OK?' he whispered.

She nodded.

Davy grabbed George into his arms. 'What *was* that?'

'Something old. Something wild. But we made it. You did it, Davy.'

As he unclipped their belts, his heart was pounding hard against his ribs.

'That saved us,' Lizzie said. 'What made you think of it?'

'I don't know. I must have seen it in some movie.'

With a roar, the wind came blasting back and snatched her. Davy grabbed for her hand, but she was gone.

'Lizzie!' he yelled. 'Lizzie! Come back!'

On the ground, lying on his belly, he felt something hard press his leg. And he remembered. Mr Bunting. The lawyer at the inn.

Some places only take the old money.

Mr Bunting's coin was still in his pocket.

Davy leaped to his feet, pulling out the coin. Throwing it high into the wind, he yelled, 'Here! Take this! Give her back!'

The wind died instantly.

'Lizzie!' She was lying out on The Grass, slumped on the ground. George raced to her, barking. As Davy ran up, he was nosing at her anxiously. 'Lizzie, are you hurt?' She seemed dazed, she was shaking. Davy helped her to her feet and up the slope to the shelter of the rocks.

'I'm fine, I'm fine,' she kept saying.

They crawled into a nook in the slabs of rock, where it was dry and silent and so dark they couldn't see each other.

'What happened? Where did you go? Where did it take you?' Davy said.

'I don't know. Please don't ask me. Get me out of here,' she said.

'Just as soon as it's light,' Davy said. He spread his jacket on the ground. 'Lie down and close your eyes. Think about the sea.'

'Please don't leave me. Not for a moment.'

'We won't leave you,' Davy said.

And he and George kept watch through the night.

Davy woke with a start. He was sitting up. He'd fallen asleep when he hadn't meant to. George's warmth was curled against him. His jacket lay empty on the ground. Lizzie was gone.

Heart racing, he scrambled out into the open, disturbing George. It was sunrise. The sky was clear. The morning was fresh against his face. The grassy mound where he stood gave him a wide view over all. 'Lizzie!' he called. To the west was a band of gleaming silver that might be the sea. To the east, he looked back on the stretch of Grass they'd crossed, last night's battleground. It rippled and waved in the gentle wind.

But Lizzie was nowhere to be seen. With panic catching in his throat, he called again, 'Lizzie! Where are you? Lizzie!' There was no reply.

A dull glint caught Davy's eye, on the ground by his boot. He crouched. It was Mr Bunting's coin. He picked it up, not able to think why it was there, what it meant. Then he realized.

He'd paid but too late. He had left everything too late. Lizzie had been too weak to fight against this place. She must have slipped away into the air while he dozed. He'd slept. He'd failed her. They'd come so far. They'd been so close.

Davy sat with his head in his hands.

Numbly, he became aware that George was urgently barking. Davy ran, clambering along the slabs of rock they'd sheltered within. It was a great long heap of stones, much larger than he'd realized. Where the rocks petered out to a shallow sprawl, he found George. And Lizzie was with him.

He threw himself beside her, breathless. 'I thought I'd lost you.'

'I'm watching the sunrise,' she said.

She turned to smile at him and Davy's heart turned in his chest. She was no more than sixteen, the soft uncurling of a hedge-rose in spring. The breeze haloed her hair around her head. In the night, she'd been like air, he'd almost lost her to the wind. Now, in the morning, she was blossoming with light. Golden freckles lay in a scatter across her nose.

'Lizzie Flint,' he said.

'Davy David.'

'I'm glad to see you.'

'I'm glad to be here,' she said.

They were silent for a time. The morning rose freshly all around them. Somewhere deep inside him, Davy felt the cleanness of the days to come. It was as if last night had blown Brownvale from his soul. 'I don't want to forget them,' he said. 'I mean, Miss Shasta and Mr Timm.'

'You won't,' Lizzie said. 'I promise. You'll carry them with you all your life.'

'We'd better get going,' he said at last.

They stood and she pointed out their direction. He'd been right. The strip of silver was the sea.

The sun rose brightly, yellow brilliant in the sky as the three of them walked into the day.

Going down a narrow farm track, they passed the open yard gate of the farmhouse. Davy could see the front wheel of a bicycle spoking out from a shed. Its butcher's boy front basket was a perfect size for George. The faint whine of a grinder came from inside the sagging barn, the only sign of life besides two ducks preening at the open kitchen door.

Davy swooped on the bike. It was a rattletrap, but the tyres were pumped. He took a moment, dodging the ducks, to leave some money on the kitchen table, then ran the bike out of the yard.

George went in the basket. Lizzie hopped up on the crossbar. As Davy swiftly cycled them away, he added taking a bike on Christmas Day to their list of crimes.

The House by the Sea

The house stood alone at the edge of the water, at the end of a narrow-track lane. It was grassy, too overgrown for the bike, so they got off and Davy pushed. George raced away. He'd been quivering with excitement since he first smelt the sea, long before either of them did.

The house, a single storey of white painted stone, was recognizably the same as in Lizzie's painting. But it was mournfully unlived in, with its shutters closed against the world. Behind it, at the end of a slope of rough grass, was a strip of white beach and the sea. The water was alive, curling to the shore, hissing up the sand and retreating. George boldly charged at the waves, in and out.

Davy had seen oceans in the movies, but in black and white, flat on the screen. He'd not expected the shock of this prowling beast. Its sun-shattered expanse dazzled him, stretching to the horizon and beyond. It was a world of sounds he didn't know. A world of unfamiliar smells. Yet his blood seemed to quicken in recognition. The endless break of waves against the land. The salty breath of the sea. The screams of wheeling white birds.

'Seagulls.' Lizzie sounded glad to see them.

She instructed him to lift the third flagstone to the left of the door. 'We always hid the spare key there.' It was rusty, as might be expected. He needed both hands to turn the lock, but at last he managed it.

'Wait.' Lizzie hung back, her arms hugging herself. 'Here's another one for your book,' she said. 'I'm afraid.' After a moment, she said, 'All right, I'm ready.'

Davy had to throw his weight against the door several times before it shuddered open. They stepped through and found themselves looking straight out to sea. A section of the back wall had collapsed. The house was open to the sky.

They stared in silence. Then, 'The roof must have fallen in,' said Lizzie. 'Of course. What did I expect? It's been years. Houses don't stand forever.'

George came running to greet them and sniffed around with huge interest as Davy began picking through the mess. Stooping and turning and lifting, buried among the plaster and rafters and roof tiles, he found the remains of a family's life. Furniture and rugs. Books and paintings. Mirrors and lamps and toys. Smashed. Broken. Faded and rotting.

'All this stuff,' he said. 'Is it yours?'

'This was our sitting room,' Lizzie said.

There was an easy chair, a lone survivor, somehow still intact. The stuffing bloomed from the rotted upholstery. 'Mother's favourite chair,' said Lizzie. 'She used to sit here and do the crossword.'

He dug a torn and faded newspaper from the mess beside it. Dated from seventy years before, it was folded to the crossword, which had been partly filled in. Davy could barely make out the pencilled letters. He showed it to Lizzie.

'She never finished this one. Two down, eight letters, *Lead a dull, inactive life*.' Lizzie thought for a moment. 'Vegetate,' she said. 'Do you hear that, Mother?'

'You just left it all.' With sudden understanding, Davy looked around him. 'You just locked the door and walked away.' He frowned. 'I don't think it's completely wrecked. This door. Where does it go?'

'Be careful,' Lizzie said, as Davy shouldered it open. 'The kitchen's that way. And the bedrooms.'

He was right. The rest of the house was still standing, just badly in need of repair.

And here, instantly, he could feel the heaviness of the past. He felt it close around him the moment he walked through the door. It was as if time itself were holding its breath.

In the kitchen, Davy got a shock. An empty coffin stood there on the floor. 'Lizzie!' he called.

She came to look at it, bemused. 'I forgot all about that. Sampson and Sons, they're a local firm.' The brass plaque screwed to the lid was engraved with her name and dates, birth and death. She touched the latter one and said, 'So much for forward planning. I was going to lie down in it and take the pills. No fuss. I made arrangements with them to pick it up. Do you think they'd give my money back?'

'Very funny,' Davy said.

As she drifted from room to room, he began opening all the shutters, and every window that wasn't stuck, and welcomed the day into the house. Everywhere was filthy with the dust of decades. He discovered the kitchen cupboards were fully stocked with dishes and glasses and pots and pans. The drawers were cluttered with cutlery, and much more besides.

He found Lizzie in her old bedroom among sketchbooks nibbled by the mice, coloured pencils and brushes in jars. There were metal trays of dried paint. A blank canvas. Her faded drawings, their corners curling, were pinned to the walls. She turned when Davy came in.

He gazed around. 'You're an artist,' he said.

'Sometimes I wonder if I might have been but . . .' She shrugged.

Davy sifted through a pile of crumbling sketches. 'These are good.' But she didn't hear him, she'd left the room. 'She was good,' he told George.

She'd made a series of charcoal drawings of a boy playing on the beach. It was the boy from her framed photograph. She'd scrawled at the bottom of one of them, *Will on the beach.* Will. So that was his name. As Davy put it down, he saw a Christmas tag on top of a stack of unopened materials. There were charcoal pencils, oil paints, a large sketchbook. The tag read *To Lizzie, with love from Mother and Will.*

She had gone across the hall to the room that had been Will's. She was standing perfectly still among his musty things. The shelves were crammed with a boy's collection of natural oddments. Stones, tiny bird skulls, feathers. A bow and arrow that he'd clearly made himself. It reminded Davy of the first time he'd met her. The ancient Miss Flint, passing her days among the bones and other things in glass cases, long forgotten by everyone but her.

He opened the shutters on another fine sea view. And, looking out at a boat sailing past, feeling the heavy silence, Davy suddenly knew. Will had died. He'd died there. The house had stopped with his death. They'd closed it up and locked the door and walked away.

'What happened to him, Lizzie?' he asked.

But she was gone. He saw her leave the house through the sitting room and head down to the beach with George.

Lizzie stood gazing out to sea, her arms hugged across her chest. She didn't look at him as he came up. 'I hired you to bring me here and you did. I'd like you to leave now, you and George. Take the money. Take all of it,' she said.

After all they'd done, everywhere they'd been. *Leave now. Take the money.* As if the past days hadn't happened. Davy saw their moments like photographs in his mind. Tipping turkeys from their crates into the orchard. Breakfast at the cafe. Riding the bus. Dancing in the moonlight in the woods. Hearing Robert Craig sing and Lizzie's tears like a fall of stars. Last night, crossing over The Grass.

Davy couldn't speak for the tightness in his throat. He scooped George into his arms and went to sit on the sand. George pressed himself against his chest, licking at his face.

Lizzie came and sat beside him, soft as thistledown.

'I'm sorry. Davy, I'm so sorry.'

'I thought we were friends,' he said.

They sat in silence. He let George go to run among the waves. Davy threw stones at the water.

At last she spoke, haltingly, with tears in her eyes. 'I've done nothing to deserve your friendship. I wouldn't blame you if you left. I don't know why I said that – no, I do know. I want to protect you from whatever's to come. This is my ending, Davy. You've hardly begun.'

'I won't leave you. We're staying, me and George.'

They were silent again.

Then Davy remembered. 'Hey,' he said. 'It's Christmas. And it's your birthday. You're eighty. How many people get to celebrate their birthday when they're dead?'

She laughed, still tearful. 'There's another one for the book. I've just had an idea,' she said. 'We'll hold a wake.'

According to Lizzie, the best kind of wake was a party in honour of the deceased involving eating and toasting the dead and sometimes music. Davy hunted through the kitchen cupboards. 'Tomato soup,' he said. 'More tomato soup. And sardines, three tins.'

As he pulled out the rusted cans she shook her head. 'Too dangerous,' she said.

But they found a bottle of rum, unopened, and a sealed tin of hard-tack crackers. Lizzie looked at them critically. 'That's a sad excuse for a feast.' She thought for a moment, then, 'Come with me,' she said.

In the little walled orchard not far from the house, the old stone walls basked in the winter sun. As Davy squeaked open the iron gate and stepped inside, he felt their warmth instantly embrace him. A faint apple smell sweetened the air. There were a few still clinging to the trees. They'd grown apples, pears, plums and berries, Lizzie told him. 'We used to make all sorts – well, Mother did. Jams and preserves, pies and cobblers.' There'd been a vegetable garden as well.

The apples were on the upper branches, too high to pick. He had to shake them down. George prudently retreated to the safety of the shore. While Davy went about jiggling the branches gently and collecting the best in his jacket, Lizzie searched around the edges for blackberries. In such a sheltered spot, warmed by the walls, 'We'd often find plenty worth eating well into December,' she said.

He realized she'd been saying *we* and *our* since arriving at the house. And he thought how every inch of it, inside and out, must be layered richly with those first years of her life.

Her next words confirmed that. 'Will hated picking blackberries. He was so impatient, always stabbing his fingers on the thorns.' It was the first time she'd said his name. She said it casually, as if Davy had known him.

Davy knew not to question her. Soon, he sensed, she would tell him more.

He took a bite of an apple. Small, a deep crimson in colour, its juicy flesh was intensely sweet. He clambered on to the wall to sit and eat it. He felt he must be in a dream with the warmth, the glittering sea, the hush of waves along the shore and the taste of apple on his lips. The air smelt of warm fruit and salt and dry grass. The sun kissed Lizzie's golden hair as she leaned and crouched in her search for berries.

Davy had taken a sheet of drawing paper from her room. He unfolded it from his pocket and began to sketch her. Her thick plait kept falling forward, getting in the way, and she'd flip it back over her shoulder, impatiently. She'd taken off her jacket and shed her shoes and stockings to go barefoot.

And Davy realized that she'd become more substantial since they arrived at the house. As if she were somehow remaking herself from the memories stored in the place.

And her character, so unforgiving, had been softer since the concert at the Rivoli. She caught his eye and smiled. 'Are you drawing me?'

The song that Robert Craig sang, how did it go?

'*Oh have you seen My Lady out in the garden . . .*' Davy had no voice for singing.

'Wrong tune, wrong words,' called Lizzie. She sang in a clear girl's voice, '*Did you not hear My Lady go down the garden singing? Blackbird and thrush were silent to hear the alleys* – Davy! Here! Blackberries!'

He hopped down from the wall and went to her. He picked the few she'd found and, like Will, got stabbed by the thorns. He tasted his first ever blackberry. It was deeply, darkly sweet.

'Not bitter?' she said.

He went to pop one in her mouth. She even opened her lips. Then they remembered. She couldn't. For she was dead. But how could she be? She seemed more alive to Davy than anyone had ever been.

Her delight at the berries was gone. Her face shadowed. 'What if we're wrong?' she said. 'What if I shouldn't be here? This place, Davy, it's so strong. If I'm caught here, if I can't go, that would be the worst, I think. To have to stay here, feeling like I do just now. Knowing that life is wonderful when it's too late to live.

I don't understand. Why am I still here?' Her voice was urgent, even angry. 'Why don't I disappear?' she demanded.

Davy had no answer to give her.

Someone had left a green rowing boat on the beach, pulled high above the tideline so it wouldn't drift away. Lizzie sat in it, looking lost. Once Davy had unloaded his fruit gleanings up at the house, he and George climbed in to join her.

'It's this waiting,' she said, 'this not knowing. I can't stand it.'

'Would it really be so bad? If you had to stay?' Davy said. 'We'd stay with you. Me and George. You wouldn't have to be alone.'

She looked at him. 'Oh, Davy,' was all she said.

They held the wake on the rough grass lawn that sloped behind the house. The orchard fruits were arranged on a plate and the tin of crackers was unsealed. With an air of solemn occasion, Davy opened the bottle of rum.

Hard-tack crackers, Lizzie said, were an acquired taste. Davy had to agree. They were dust dry. He alternated bites of cracker with bites of apple to try and ease them down but it didn't help much. Despite his hunger, he could only manage two. He finished his meal with some berries. 'What comes next?' he said. 'Wait, I know. A toast to the dead.'

He went to splash rum into a mug but Lizzie stopped him.

'Not so fast,' she said. 'May I remind you that you're thirteen years old? That's far too young for liquor. I can't allow it.'

'Are you forbidding me?' He felt a smile begin to creep across his face.

'Most certainly,' she said, with primly folded arms.

She was way up on her high horse, positively oozing Miss Flint-style disapproval. Throughout the afternoon, her journey back into girlhood had continued. It was so gradual, so imperceptible, the shedding of years. In front of his eyes, without him noticing, she'd become a flat-chested, skinny child.

Davy began to laugh.

'What?' she said.

'It's funny. You talk like you're still eighty but you can't be more than ten.'

'That's as may be,' she said. 'Technically, I'll always be your elder. And drinking in the day is just louche. You may have a sip.'

With a careless hand, Davy took a mouthful. Instantly he was coughing as the rum seared a fire path down his throat. Now it was Lizzie who was laughing. Once he'd recovered, Davy raised his mug and said, 'To the memory of Miss Elizabeth Flint. Famous drinker of Manhattan cocktails, turkey rustler and all-round thief.'

She nodded in gracious acknowledgement.

'What next?' he said.

'People take it in turns to talk about the deceased, sharing stories that show them in a good light,' said Lizzie. 'It's customary to bend the truth or even lie outright. To praise virtues they never possessed in life. There's none so admired as the recently deceased, none so charitable as the person worried what might be said of them when their time comes.'

'All right,' he said. 'Should I go first?'

'No.' Her smile was gone. 'I knew her best.'

Davy would always remember that. How Lizzie told her story as if it had happened to someone else. It must have been the only way she could bring herself to tell it. He saw her rolling back time to when everything stopped. He saw it in the flicker of her eyelids, the biting of her lip. She spoke the bare bones, that was all. In later years, when Davy had grown in the world, he would put flesh on those bones and understand so much more than she told him.

'No lies. No bending the truth. Just a story,' she said. She took a deep breath and began.

'It was family tradition to sail around the point to the harbour on Christmas Day. That year, that day, there was some delay with their mother. They were forever having to wait for her, she never could keep to time. The two children had been bickering, about nothing in particular, as brothers and sisters are inclined to do. And Will had been badgering their mother to let him go out in the dinghy by himself.' Lizzie paused for a moment, then continued. 'He was only seven, but so strong willed. He'd never be told, especially by his sister. So, they ignored each other while they waited for her on the beach. Neither one willing to give ground, to be the one to make the first move back to friendly relations. Christmas Day. Lizzie never liked it, she thought it took everyone's attention from her birthday. You care deeply about things like that when you're a child.'

She stopped. She'd rushed through some bits, picked her way slowly through others.

'It's OK,' said Davy.

'Must I go on?' she whispered.

He nodded.

Lizzie stood, as if she had to be on her feet to tell the rest. She began to pace. 'She saw what Will was doing. She saw him wade out and swim to the buoy where the boat was moored. She saw him climb in. She yelled to him that he wasn't allowed, he'd be in trouble. But she knew him, knew what he was like. She knew very well he'd take that as a challenge. She should have gone and got their mother right away. She should have.'

'How old were – how old was Lizzie?' said Davy.

'Ten. She was ten. Old enough to know the danger and not to bait him.' She stopped again. 'I can't,' she said.

'Yes, you can. Go on,' Davy said.

She took a shaky breath. 'He was small for his age. It was an old boat, heavy wood with a heavy canvas sail, too much for Will. His friends were all older, bigger boys, much stronger. She knew, Lizzie knew how it stung his pride that he couldn't sail out with them. The only wonder was he hadn't tried it before. He managed to raise the sail but he wasn't strong enough to hold it and tie it off. The sail came down – clattering – it fell so quickly. It knocked him overboard. Lizzie screamed for their mother and swam out. But they couldn't find him. No one could.'

'But they searched for him,' said Davy.

'For days,' she said. 'For weeks, up and down the coast. Word travelled quickly. People miles away searched. Everyone looked for him, by water, on foot. All the beaches and coves and caves, every little rocky island. At high tide and low tide. They went out every day, Lizzie and her mother. The sea turned wild that winter.'

'He was never found,' said Lizzie.

'Then they left?' said Davy.

'He was gone, but he was everywhere. It was unbearable. After some months, they closed the shutters, locked the doors and moved away. They lived small, closed-in lives and blamed themselves, especially Lizzie. She was older than him. She was bigger. She could have stopped him.'

'You don't know that,' Davy said. 'You don't know.'

She looked at him for the first time since she'd started speaking. 'I called him a baby,' she said. 'I knew the mood he was in. The only thing I can say for myself is I made sure I could never make a mistake like that again.' She began to walk towards the water. 'The wake's over.'

'What about my turn?' he called.

'You don't get one.' She stood where the waves broke around her feet.

She'd never told anyone before. Davy didn't know how he knew, he just did. And now he knew why she hadn't married Robert Craig. Why she'd ended up caged in the closed museum.

Davy went to stand beside Lizzie, with his bare feet in the sea. Not to say anything to try and make things right, no words could do that. But he could stand with her, as a friend, so he did.

As Davy stood there, pondering what she'd said, something began to stir within him. 'It happened when you were ten,' he said slowly. 'I'd say you're ten now and you have been for a time.' Then it hit him. 'Lizzie,' he said. 'You're not getting any younger. You've stopped.'

She stared at him. 'You're right.' Her face brightened for a moment, then went dark. 'So why am I still here?'

'I don't know,' he said.

With a smothered cry, she turned and quickly walked away.

The sky was endless. The sea was vast. Davy was small and had no answers.

He and George walked down the beach a way. Davy picked up a stick and, without purpose, began to draw in the sand. When he realized the shape it was taking, his interest sharpened. He collected various sticks and stones and, using them and his hands, put a boy and a girl in the boat he'd drawn. He set it on water and made the sail billow with the wind. He put a dog in the boat for good measure. There were no angels looking down on them, no angels passing by. For wings, he put seagulls in the sky.

As he finished and stepped back, Lizzie came to look. 'It's the dog in your photograph,' he said.

'Angus,' she said. 'George reminds me of him.'

'It's for you. Happy birthday. Merry Christmas,' he said.

She smiled. 'It's perfect,' she said.

While they stood there, the wind was rising. It began

to scatter his picture to the air. 'Oh no, come back!' Lizzie cried.

They chased the flying sand along the beach.

The sun was setting. Its firestorm blazed the horizon. Lizzie suddenly stopped and looked out to sea. She went very still.

'What is it?' Davy shaded his eyes, but the sun was blinding.

Then Lizzie began to run.

And Davy ran after her, yelling, 'Lizzie! Wait! Wait for me!'

L izzie ran to the green rowing boat pulled up on the shore and tried to haul it towards the water, forgetting that she couldn't. When she shouted, 'Help me, Davy!' he was already there.

He dragged the boat down the sand, saying, 'What, Lizzie? What? Is this it?'

'I don't know, all I know is you have to take me out there.'

She and George jumped in the moment they reached the water's edge. Davy walked the boat out a little further, soaking his trousers and boots, then scrambled aboard.

'There's a life jacket under the seat. Put it on,' Lizzie said.

He took up the oars as she told him and began to row. Awkward at first, clunking them and splashing water everywhere, he soon got the hang of how to hold the boat steady. He settled to a rhythm and set a course out to sea.

'Faster,' she said. 'Faster. Put your back into it.'

He did, glancing over his shoulder. And he saw what she saw. A black outline against the red face of the sun. 'Is that a boat?'

She didn't answer. Her gaze was fixed on it. He rowed, his chest burning with the effort. He checked again. It was a sailboat, he could clearly see the outline.

'Hurry,' she kept saying. 'Hurry, Davy.'

Rowing and rowing, he *had* to be closing the distance between them. And the sailboat didn't seem to move. Yet it was as if he were rowing on the spot.

'We'll never reach it,' said Lizzie.

Davy rested, breathing hard, nodding. His hands were stinging, blistering raw from the oars. 'What should we do?'

'I don't know, how can I know? I've never done this before. Help me, Davy. Please.' She began to cry.

He took up the oars again and began to row with all the strength he had, grunting with the effort, bracing his feet. They surged forward, slicing through the calm water.

'It's no good,' she said at last. 'We can't reach it. We'll never reach it.'

Davy stopped.

George was anxiously squirming between them,

trying to lick them into happiness. 'Oh, George,' said Lizzie. 'What will I do?'

They sat in silence. Davy bent over the oars. He could not bear to meet her eyes. After everything, at this last moment, he'd failed her. 'I'm sorry,' he said.

'It's not your fault. You've done all you could and more.' After a moment, she said, 'I'm not meant to go, am I? Yes, that's it. I'm meant to stay here and make atonement.' She whispered the last word.

'Atonement?' said Davy.

'Make amends for what I did.'

He thought. Then he said, 'You didn't let yourself really live. Seventy years. Doesn't that count?'

They sat in silence, drifting. The water gently lapped at the boat. And suddenly Davy knew. He urgently knew. 'Lizzie, if that's Will out there, he's come for you. Don't you see? He doesn't want you to stay. He doesn't want your atonement, he doesn't need it. *You're* the one keeping yourself here. You, Lizzie. You're the one.'

'Me.' She stared at him.

'*Wait for me, Will. I'm on my way.* Say it, Lizzie.'

'Wait for me, Will,' she whispered. 'I'm on my way.'

Davy picked up the oars and began to row again. 'Louder,' he said. 'He has to hear you.'

'Wait for me, Will. I'm on my way.'

'Louder,' he said. 'Shout it out.'

'Wait for me, Will,' she shouted. 'Wait for me. I'm on my way.'

'That's it.' Davy rowed with renewed strength. He began to shout with her. 'Wait for her, Will. She's on her way.'

George added his voice, barking and barking.

'There's the boat,' she yelled. 'I can see it. There it is!'

And as the rowing boat surged forward, from beneath the water, all around them, great silver creatures began to leap. Their sleek bodies arced high into the air. 'Look at those fish!' Davy cried.

Lizzie was smiling. 'Not fish,' she said. 'They're dolphins. A pod of dolphins!'

There were five or six of them. They leaped around the boat, again and again, as if they were urging Davy on. He rowed, filled with a joy he'd never felt before, laughing for no reason he could think of. 'What are they doing? Why are they here?'

George was under Davy's seat, quivering with fright, looking with fascination.

Lizzie suddenly grabbed the sides of the boat. Her eyes were wide. 'Stop,' she said. 'Davy, stop!'

He paused, panting.

'They're here for me,' she said.

The sea was still as a pond. The dolphins frisked around the boat, surfacing and falling, blowing air through the holes in their heads.

'I know what I have to do. I'm going with them.' She smiled, trembling with eagerness.

Davy's voice stuck in his throat. 'I can't say goodbye. Not to you.'

'Then we won't,' she said. 'No goodbyes. Just thank you.'

She hugged George. Then she hugged Davy. And her arms, as she hugged him, felt like a circling of the air. She smelt of sun and the sweetness of apples. He whispered that he'd remember her all his life.

She smiled at him. It was a smile of such radiant expectation that he thought she knew what would happen to her next. Time stopped. His heart stood still. Then Lizzie shattered into light. Davy stared, breathless with wonder. She was now millions of tiny points of the whitest light he had ever seen. She was too bright to look at. He had to glance away. When he looked back, Lizzie was gone.

But the dolphins were on the move. With sudden urgency, they swam off. The pod sliced through the water, leaping, their silver bodies gleaming in the waning light, as they headed for the boat that waited there.

Davy held George on his lap and watched them go. He felt his heart aching in his chest.

The sun was dying with a last riot flare, blinding Davy with its dazzle. The sailboat was a shadow against its blaze.

But, shading his eyes, he thought he saw her. He thought he saw the dolphins reach the boat – that someone on deck leaned out to help her climb aboard – that the two of them then turned in his direction – and Davy thought, he believed, that he saw them wave.

He raised his hands high in farewell, just in case.

They stayed until the sun slipped into the sea, he and George. Then, in the twilight, Davy rowed back to shore.

The sun was out when Davy woke the morning after Christmas Day. He and George had stayed up late, missing Lizzie, not knowing what to do. They'd sat for a long time, just looking at the stars. And he thought how she'd said that if she found herself among the stardust, she would blink down at him so he'd know where she was. But every star in the sky had been blinking. When at last they hit the floor in Lizzie's old room, exhausted though Davy was, he couldn't sleep. Counting off the hours by the distant chimes of some church clock, he'd finally slept just as dawn was breaking.

He felt the sharp edge of something digging into his back. It was a small metal trunk. He sat up, yawning, and unclasped it. It was full of books, Lizzie's books from her childhood. She'd written her name on the flyleaves in a large looping hand. On top lay *The Adventures of Tom Sawyer*. It was from the local library and long overdue. She'd borrowed it seventy years ago.

'That'll be some fine,' he said to George.

Davy took the book outside and sat in the sunshine. It really ought to be returned. He had no immediate plans. He could stay until the library opened after the holidays. If the librarian was anything like Mr Timm, they'd love to hear the story of why *Tom Sawyer* was overdue. In the meantime, he might as well read it. Nibbling an apple for his breakfast, Davy began.

He was deeply engrossed when George began to bark down at the water's edge. Only now did Davy notice the green rowing boat wasn't on the beach. It had been taken out and was heading in to shore. The rower shipped the oars and jumped into the shallows to pull it in. Davy ran to meet him and help him with the boat. It contained several pots of clacking lobsters.

Unsmiling, the man nodded his thanks. He glanced up at the house with its open shutters. Broad and tall, with a reddish beard and a head of thick straight hair, his grey eyes pierced Davy. 'And who might you be?' he said.

'We're friends of Miss Flint's,' said Davy.

'Lizzie Flint? Here?' said the man. 'She's still alive?'

Davy hesitated. Then, 'No,' he said. 'She's . . . gone west. It's just us.'

The man's stern face softened, just a little. 'What brings you here?'

'She told me so many stories,' said Davy. 'I wanted to see the house for myself.'

'It's a sad old place,' said the man. 'Not much to see. That business with the boy was tragic. It happened before I was born, but my folks would talk about it. These things stay in the memory of small places. We're the nearest neighbours. I'm Matthew Blye.'

'I'm Davy. This is George.'

They shook hands. As Mr Blye scratched George's ears, he looked at Davy with narrowed eyes. 'Just the two of you, you said?'

Davy nodded.

'It's just . . . when I was coming in just now, I thought I saw . . .' He shook his head. 'Ah, never mind. It's this old house,' he said. The sea was like that too, he told Davy. It sometimes made you see things that weren't there. 'Are you camping here for a bit?'

'Maybe,' Davy said. 'If that's all right.'

'Please yourself. But if it's quiet you're wanting, you're out of luck,' said Mr Blye. 'I fish from here most days and my lot are always tearing up and down. We're cooking lobster on the beach today, our Christmas tradition. You're welcome to join us. Nothing fancy, but – ah, here they come.'

Then, in a hurricane of shouting and laughter, Mr

Blye's family were upon them. Davy held George as the four children – three girls and a boy – came rushing around the house towards them. Each one bore some precious cargo for the feast. They talked loudly, at top speed, overlapping one another, eager to tell their father what they had. The box of best plates and cutlery wrapped in the special Christmas cloth. The basket full of warm loaves just out of the oven. The big iron cooking pot for the lobsters.

Mr Blye raised his voice above the babble. 'You'll frighten our guests off. This is Davy and George.'

They all said hello, wished Davy *Merry Christmas* and the smallest one, a toddling girl of three or so, dropped her tiny load and ran at Mr Blye. He swung her up into his arms, saying, 'This little gingersnap is Dot. Dot, say hello to Davy.'

'No,' she said.

'She says no to everything,' said Mr Blye. As he swung her down again, Tom came over and Mr Blye said to him, 'Good to have another fellow on our side, eh?'

'Me and Dad are outnumbered,' said Tom. He smiled at Davy. Davy smiled at him. Tom looked to be around his age.

Then Mrs Blye was there, too, and her mother who lived with them. And all the Blyes were so welcoming and easy and including that Davy couldn't have hung back even if he'd wanted to. Before he knew it, he was combing the beach helping to collect driftwood for the fire and building it with Tom to Pip's instructions. She was ten and clearly worshipped her brother. Her full name was Philippa, but no one was allowed to call her that, not ever. She warned Davy that anyone who did could expect a fight.

'Don't think she doesn't mean it,' said Tom. 'She gave me a famous black eye once.'

She asked Davy where he lived. He paused and then he answered, 'I guess I'm between places,' he said.

Just as the pot was coming to the boil ready for the lobsters, George went barking to the front of the house. Davy and the Blye children ran after him to see why. They watched a dusty saloon car bump up the track to the house. It parked and the driver, a man in a rumpled suit, got out and stretched. To Davy's astonishment, it was Mr Bunting, the lawyer, last seen snoring on the bar at the New Inn.

'Ah, here you are,' he said to Davy. 'Merry Christmas, all. I'm Bunting.' His hair was still wild around his head, his face was still kind and open. He smiled at Davy with his clear blue eyes. 'You're a hard man to find. I've had the police on your trail.'

'The police!' Tom looked at Davy with the utmost respect.

'That was you?' Davy said.

Mr Bunting unloaded two paper grocery bags from the back seat. 'I brought provisions. I figured the cupboards would be bare.'

'We have loads,' cried Pip. 'Come and see.'

Davy made an awkward hash of introducing him to the Blyes.

'We're old friends.' Mr Bunting winked at Davy.

Mrs Blye said he'd arrived just in time. Then the lobsters were set to boiling and that Christmas feast on the beach – lobster with melted butter that went running down their chins – was more delicious than anything Davy could have imagined. Despite that, he couldn't really enjoy it. Mr Bunting had gone to great lengths to track him down. He was a lawyer. It must mean that Davy was in trouble.

When they'd finished eating Mr Bunting said quietly, only for Davy's ears, 'Why do you suppose I had the police looking for you?'

Davy's bread stuck in his throat. He swallowed. 'The turkey truck. The bicycle. The police car,' he said.

'As your lawyer, I advise you to stop there,' said Mr Bunting. 'What I don't hear, I can't know. Let's take a walk.' He raised his voice. 'That was splendid, Mrs Blye, thank you. Would you excuse us?'

They walked along the beach with George. 'You're my lawyer now?' Davy said. 'Will they arrest me?'

Mr Bunting just said, 'It's years since I was at the beach.' He stopped to fill his lungs with the heady, salty air. He sat on the ground, removed his shoes and socks and rolled his trouser legs to the knee. 'Think I'll go for a paddle.' He took a white envelope from his inside jacket pocket and handed it to Davy. 'Merry Christmas, kid,' he said, and wandered off, whistling.

Davy's name was printed on the envelope in shaky letters. Inside, he found two sheets of writing paper folded together. The first was a note. Just a few lines. It had clearly taken great effort for her to write it. It was dated from that first night at the New Inn, the night she died.

Dear Davy,

I've been solitary for a very long time. The past few hours, I've lived more and felt more than I have for many years. That's thanks to you.

Be unafraid, Davy David. For the time we are given is rare and brief.

Fly on your own wings.

Your friend,

Elizabeth Flint

He unfolded the second paper. It was in someone else's writing. Again, it was dated that first night at the New Inn.

I, Elizabeth Flint, being of sound mind –

Davy sat abruptly on the ground. He had to take a breath before he could read on. She'd left him the house. She'd left him money. Everything to him. All she owned. There were some furthermores, but that was it. Mr Bunting would oversee the arrangements. The will was in his handwriting. It had been witnessed by the New Inn's barman and the kitchen porter. She must have called for them after Davy left her that night.

He swiped at the hot tears spilling down his cheeks. George climbed on to his lap and licked his face.

Mr Bunting's arms were wide open, a shoe in each hand. The waves broke around his bare feet. As if he felt Davy's eyes on him, he turned around, smiling, and waggled his shoes in delight. 'Merry Christmas!' he shouted. Then he threw his shoes into the sea.

'Merry Christmas!' cried Davy. 'Come on, George!'

They raced back to the house, to *his* house. Davy found a hammer and some tacks in a kitchen drawer. He chose the sturdiest wall of the sitting room and hung

Lizzie's painting of the house in pride of place. Below it, he tacked the torn-out painting from his pocket. The steady-eyed warrior and his hound gazed at Davy. 'We did it,' he told them. 'Thanks to you. Say thank you, George.' George barked three times.

From the rubble, Davy hauled out a little table that he'd seen. He set it upright and put the photograph on top. Of Will in his shorts and Lizzie in her cotton dress, at the front door of the house with their dog, Angus, on a summer's day.

When he turned around, Tom and Pip were watching with interest. 'Mr Bunting told us.' said Pip. 'This is your place now. You're going to live here.'

Davy looked around. 'Yes,' he said. 'It's my place.'

'Dad figures we can get the roof back on by the New Year,' said Tom. 'After the lobster, we always have a game of football on the beach here. Will you play?'

'I have to do something first.'

'We'll wait for you.'

Davy took the large sketchpad from Lizzie's room, given to her on that long ago Christmas. He took the unopened box of charcoal pencils. They'd been waiting and waiting in the silence of the house and at last, at last they would be used. He took them down to the shore and began to draw. He made the sea and the sunset and the gleaming bodies of leaping dolphins. A girl with long hair swam with them into the setting sun. It was rough, but he knew he would improve.

Mr Bunting strolled up with rolled sleeves and sandy feet. 'She said you were an artist.'

'Yes,' said Davy. 'Oh!' He'd suddenly remembered. He dug in his pocket for Mr Bunting's coin. 'You were right. Some places only take the old money. Thanks for the loan.'

Mr Bunting smiled a quizzical little smile. 'So, she got off all right? Any problems?' He raised an eyebrow.

Davy stared at him with dawning wonder. As he understood, he began to smile. 'Nothing I couldn't manage,' he said. 'Here's your coin.'

'Keep it handy,' said Mr Bunting. 'You just never know.'

He made himself comfortable on the sand, lying back with his arms behind his head. He closed his eyes and Davy carried on with his drawing. He was so quiet, Davy thought he must have fallen asleep. Until, in a drowsy voice, with his eyes still closed, he said, '*And to die is different from what any one supposed*. Walt Whitman said that. What would you say?'

'I'd say he might be right,' said Davy.

'He just might,' said Mr Bunting.

Davy could feel the house waking behind them. The day was the finest he'd ever known. Millions of diamonds danced upon the sea.

There was a trick of the light that bright day. It was later on, when they were all playing football. Mr Blye kicked the ball down the beach and Davy chased along the sand after it. As he scooped up the ball, that's when he saw her.

She was playing there among the rocks in her thin cotton dress. Her feet were bare, her hair hung forward in a careless plait. She looked up and saw him. And she smiled. Then, as if she'd heard someone calling her name, she turned away quickly and was gone.

He stood, staring at where she'd been, but not for long. Tom shouted for him to hurry and George came barking up to get him.

Davy turned away and ran back to their game.

The sun blazed its joy down. The waves came and went. And the seagulls soared on wings of white fire, high above them in the clear blue air.

Acknowledgements

This book came to life thanks to the loving tyranny of my agent, Gillie Russell; I am deeply grateful. Thanks always to Paul Stansall, who picks me up, dusts me off and keeps me going. And thanks, as ever, to Sophie McKenzie, Gaby Halberstam, Sharon Flockhart, Melanie Edge and Julie Mackenzie. Thank you also to Venetia Gosling and the excellent folk at Macmillan Children's Books, Jean Feiwel of Feiwel & Friends, and Amy Black and the team at Doubleday Canada for their wholehearted support.

In the realm of signs, portents and synchronicities, I acknowledge the following with gratitude: the abiding spirits of Philip Van Doren Stern, Frank Capra and James Stewart; Ian Duff and his dog, Boycie, who delivered a timely nudge from the universe; Katharine Pollen for saying the right thing at the right time; and the woman I met in a California bookshop, who sees the dead who walk among us every day.

The fragment of poetry that Mr Bunting quotes is from 'Song of Myself' by Walt Whitman.

Appendix of Movies

The Phantom of the Opera (1925)
Directors: Rupert Julian, Lon Chaney
Stars: Lon Chaney, Mary Philbin, Norman Kelly

The Great Mancini (1930)
Director: King Cortez
Stars: Fidor Stark, Sidney Sinclair
(Well-informed opinion holds that even the most
determined film scholar will fail to unearth any
evidence of *The Great Mancini*.)

Flying Down to Rio (1933)
Director: Thornton Freeland
Stars: Dolores del Rio, Gene Raymond, Paul Roulien,
Fred Astaire, Ginger Rogers

Top Hat (1935)
Director: Mark Sandrich
Stars: Fred Astaire, Ginger Rogers, Edward
Everett Horton

Now, Voyager (1942)
Director: Irving Rapper
Stars: Bette Davis, Paul Heinreid, Claude Rains

It's a Wonderful Life (1946)
Director: Frank Capra
Stars: James Stewart, Donna Reed, Lionel Barrymore

The Ghost and Mrs Muir (1947)
Director: Joseph L Mankiewicz
Stars: Gene Tierney, Rex Harrison, George Sanders

Sunset Boulevard (1950)
Director: Billy Wilder
Stars: William Holden, Gloria Swanson, Erich
von Stroheim

About the Author

Moira Young was an actress and opera singer before becoming a writer. She is the author of the critically acclaimed Dustlands trilogy: *Blood Red Road*, *Rebel Heart* and *Raging Star*, published in thirty countries. *Blood Red Road*, her debut novel, won a host of prizes, including the Costa Children's Book Award, the BC Book Prize, the Cybils Award for Fantasy and Science Fiction and Le Prix des Incorruptibles. A native of Vancouver, Canada, she now lives in the UK.

www.moirayoung.com